STUART BRAY'S
VIOLENCE ON THE MEEK 4
SACROSANCTITY

WARNING:

This is EXTREME HORROR. If you are easily offended, I advise you to put this book down and check out a copy of Bambi and Friends from your local library. This book wasn't written with your delicate sensitivities in mind. This book contains extremely graphic depictions of death, murder, and sexual assault on men, women, and dead animals. If any of this sounds like too much, put this book down, pat yourself on the back, and congratulate yourself for at least giving it a shot. For those of you that stick it out until the end, I commend you, I thank you, and I appreciate you.

For all those temporary friends. The ones that you once worked with but haven't seen since then. I haven't forgotten the best of you. Ron, Mike, Joel, Ronnie. B, Wayne, Sam, Matt, Mark, Eric, and Audie Wilson. Thank you all for making a boring workday... bearable.

CONTENTS

BEFORE THE MEEK

THE SWEET TASTE OF chrome filled my mouth, kick starting my senses. My path of destruction had ended, and it all lay before me in a neat little stack. The pencil I had used to write the entire fucking thing rolled off the table, hitting the cement floor. I was a fucking legend at this point, a fucking scary story to keep children awake in their beds at night, staring at the shadows on the closet door. Franny was dead, Mary-Ann was dead; they were *all* fucking dead. I smiled, biting down softly on the barrel of the 357 Magnum.

"Do it, faggot! I bet you won't." I laughed at the voice in my head, always trying to taunt me.

"Dying is for the weak." I pulled the gun from my mouth, sliding my tongue down the barrel, almost to taunt the thing that almost ended my miserable existence. I aimed the gun towards the ceiling, firing a shot that made my fucking ears ring. It would have been an absolute fucking shame for someone as talented as me to die in the prime of their life. But what should I do with myself? I couldn't go on another full-blown killing spree, I couldn't risk being put down like a fucking dog, not like I was in the nuthouse the day I went to visit my whore of a mother.

Those cocksuckers pumped me full of bullets, but still didn't get the job done. Wasn't like the cunts didn't do any damage. My body was completely fucked. I remember lying in that hospital bed. That old prick that had spent years tracking me down, staring down at me with a smile.

"You're all I've known for the past ten years, you know that? I've given up everything in pursuit of *you*." The old man was starting to bore me with his pathetic whining. I wanted to ram my fist down his throat and pull his asshole out through his mouth.

"This may come as a surprise to you, because it certainly doesn't make any damned sense to me." The old cop looked around the empty room, making sure none of the nurses were around to hear what he had to say. He leaned forward, pushing the point of his elbow into my chest. The pain was fucking glorious. If my fucking jaw hadn't been wired shut, I would have eaten his fucking tongue.

"I'm going to let you heal up enough so that you can just barely walk. Then, I'm going to turn my back and let you walk right out that door, you hear me? I'll make sure no other officers are on guard. I'll make sure no one sees your sick, twisted ass walking out as a '*temporarily*' free man."

I laughed under the wires holding my jaw shut. I was the only thing this worthless old fuck had left; his only fucking reason to keep living. He was going to let me go, like an injured bear being freed from a trap, only to be hunted while wounded.

The old fuck wasn't kidding either, he let me walk right out the fucking door four weeks later. The physical therapist did a bang-up job helping me to walk again. This little blonde bitch couldn't have been older than twenty, perfect little tits, a firm, tight ass. I got myself in a little trouble after I ran my hand up her skirt to check and see if her pussy was smiling for me. The officers on duty beat the holy fuck out of me for a solid five minutes. I blew the little tease a kiss as she cried in the corner of the room.

I turned to give the tired old cop one final look as I limped down the hallway. He nodded, a bead of sweat dripping down his wrinkled forehead. I wondered if he knew that he was my father. Hell, I couldn't believe it myself. I was half expecting to catch a bullet to the back of the head before I made it through the hospital doors, but the old fuck didn't move an inch. I reached into the pocket of the blue jeans the old fuck tossed at me before I was even out of bed.

"You, crazy old fuck." I said with a smile, flipping through the stack of cash that had been left for me. I looked around the parking lot, knowing I needed to get as far away from this fucking place as I could. I ended up coming across a woman loading groceries in the back of a minivan, her bratty little girl screaming about some toy she wasn't allowed to get. As soon as the bitch strapped her little angel in the backseat, I wrapped my arm around her neck, then put my free hand over her screaming fucking mouth.

"Don't fucking scream! If you make a peep, I'll stab your cunt daughter in the fucking face!"

The mother nodded. My cock grew hard against her ass. My entire fucking body throbbed in agony as I pushed the woman into the passenger's seat of the minivan, then an ear-piercing scream came from the backseat. I turned to the little snot faced bitch, tears streaming down her rosy, red cheeks. "Shut your fucking mouth! Keep crying and I'll slit mommy's eyelids open!"

The little brat sucked up her tears, burying her face in a tiny red jacket next to her boaster seat. "Good girl." I smiled, wondering what in the hell I would cut this bitch with when the time came.

"Please, please don't hurt my daughter. Do whatever you want with me, just let me drop my daughter off somewhere safe. Please, I beg you."

I flicked a little wooden cross that dangled from the rearview mirror before grabbing the cunt by her cheaply done hair.

"Please! I'm sorry!"

I leaned in to lick her neck. Her body tensed up at my touch. "What's wrong? Does your faggot husband *not* touch you like this? He must not know how to make you feel good, huh?" I reached over to slide my hand up the woman's dark pink blouse, pinching as hard as I could on thick round nipple. The church bitch let out a cry of pain, clenching her jaw hard enough that I could hear her fucking teeth crack. "Drive me out to the old steel mill, the one a few miles outside of town."

I caught my reflection in the rearview mirror, I had grown a thick, scruffy beard, and my hair hung down past my ears.

"Please, let my daughter out of the car before we go. I promise to not scream."

I was becoming irritated that the fucking grocery getter wasn't pulling the fuck out of the parking lot yet. I guess this fucking stuck up cunt wasn't taking me seriously. I punched her as hard as I could in the side of the face, causing myself insurmountable pain in the process. The brat in the backseat started screaming again, I reached back and punched her in the nose, causing blood to pour from her nostrils like an open faucet. I grabbed her by one of the ponytails that bounced joylessly on her little shoulder. "Shut your fucking cocksucker, you little pubescent cunt." I pulled with all my strength, ripping the ponytail right off the little girl's head. I guess the pain caused her to pass out. Her head fell to the side, cracking loudly against the window.

"Look at this!" I smacked the mother in the head before stuffing her daughter's pigtail in her wide-open mouth. "Drive this fucking van, or the *next thing* down your throat will be her still-beating-heart!"

Needless to say, the prissy little bitch got the message. The drive took longer than I expected, especially considering the amount of pain that I was in. Every goddamned muscle in my body ached, my head pounded like someone had dropped a ten-pound weight on it from a three-story building.

"A pencil and paper, do you have it?" I asked the woman, now fighting to keep my eyes open. The bitch side-eyed me like I was fucking stupid. I reached my hand back up her shirt, being a bit more aggressive this time.

"In my daughter's school- school bag, in the backseat." I couldn't help but laugh as the Christ loving cunt started sobbing again. Once we finally reached my destination, the sun started to set. The factory was dark and had been abandoned since the late seventies; the perfect spot to lie low. "Please, sir. Please can I take my daughter home now? I did what you asked, please let us go."

I tilted my seat back, winching in pain. I wished so badly that I had a gun, it would save me from the pulled stitches that I knew were already fucked. I decided that I would ride into the next town tomorrow to retrieve one somehow. Something with a nice kick to it, but easy to conceal.

"I want you to climb in the back seat with your kid." I nodded towards the back of the van, where the little girl had now woken up. "Climb back there and buckle yourself up."

The mother stammered for a moment; her hands shook like a retard who had just been frightened.

"Get back there, or I'll just kill you both separately. Your fucking choice, bitch." After smacking the bitch around a little, she finally climbed into the back seat with her stupid fucking kid.

"Now look." I fought to turn myself in the front seat. "I'm going to kill you both with whatever tire changing tool that I'm certain you have in the back of this piece of shit van." The mother and daughter's cries sounded like a sick litter of puppies in a cardboard box. In the back of the van I found a spare tire, a cheap and shitty car jack, and a rusted crowbar.

"That'll do," I sighed, walking back around to the van's sliding door.

"Please! Please don't do this!" The mother wrapped her arms around her daughter, pulling her face into her chest. Something about this moment reminded me of my childhood, it reminded me of how Mary-Ann's mother fought for her until the bitter end. I beat the church cunt in the head nine or ten times before she went limp. The little girl screamed so loudly before I cracked her skull that I was afraid she would attract a pack of coyotes. I dragged both corpses from the backseat, which was fucking stupid on my part.

"Help me!"

"What the fuck!?" I jumped back as the little girl sat up in the tall grass, her left eye bulging from the socket. I rammed the straight end of the crowbar down her throat, then pushed as hard as I could. "Fucking kids, Jesus fucking Christ!"

I took a deep breath as I dropped the bodies into a large, rusted oil barrel on the far side of the building. I would have to fight the urge to come back out here and fuck one of their corpses. The van fit nicely under a small overhead, I covered it with an old, blue tarp. "I have to lay down, I fucking have to." I dropped to my knees inside one of the cramped offices on the lower level, using a stack of papers as my pillow.

Two days later, I grabbed myself a .357 Magnum from a sporting goods store in the next town over. The kike looking faggot wearing bottlecap glasses standing behind the counter told me that there was a waiting period, so I slit his throat with a broken shard of glass behind the store on his lunch break. Once I made It back to the factory, something inside me forced me to sit my ass down and write out my life story. I wrote about my childhood, my bitch mother, meeting Franny, even the ten fucking years that I hid out in a shithole cabin in the middle of nowhere. I wrote about killing Mary-Ann, I went into great detail about how, later in life, I wanted to fuck her. The supermarket, the obsessed cop, the fucking pig farm, it was all in there, I titled it 'Violence on the Meek.'

It had been a few years, and I had moved from shithole to shithole, never staying in one place for too long. Not once in all that time did I catch the tiniest glimpse of the man I believed to be my father; the man who let me walk away.

There was a nationwide manhunt for the longest time, but it eventually went under the radar after some little dipshit went on a killing spree in his hometown sometime in 2002. I thought long and hard about where I wanted to be, and 'who' exactly I wanted to be now that my legend had grown, now that it had spilled over into suburban America. People loved me, they worshiped me, and I would use every fucking bit of *that* to my advantage.

Chapter One

FARMGIRL1990

July 15th, 2009

"IF YOU KEEP SUCKING it like that, I'll never cum." Mike raised his head from Nevin's lap, strings of spit dangling from his bottom lip. "We've talked about how to suck a cock, haven't we?" Mike nodded his head in embarrassment. Nevin knew he was being too hard on someone he considered a *'sidepiece'*, but the little twink couldn't suck a dick to save his life.

"I'm trying to do the things we talked about, it's just difficult to do this in a car." Mike protested, wiping the spit from his lip, swallowing a bit of the pre-cum he had managed to squeeze out of Nevin's dick slit.

Nevin rolled his eyes, shoving Mike's head back into his exposed crotch.

"You're going to have to tug on it a little to get it hard again. Honestly, I'll be surprised if you're able to accomplish that in the little amount of time we have." Nevin squeezed tightly on the back of Mike's neck. "Maybe if I pretend you don't want to suck my cock, maybe I'll imagine that I'm mouth raping some twink faggot that I picked up on the side of the road." Nevin closed his eyes, having to stroke his own cock for a moment to get it ready for Mike's throat.

"Fuck you, Nevin! I'm not going to be treated like some fucking whore that you picked up off the street!" Mike jerked away, leaning back in the passenger's seat of Nevin's Ford Focus. He crossed his arms to show that he was pouting.

Nevin sighed, grabbing ahold of his cock, stroking up and down, trying to finish himself off.

"It looks like you don't even need me." Mike huffed, kicking his feet around in the floorboard like a spoiled child.

"Just shut the fuck up for a minute so I can finish. I'm imagining that someone interesting has my dick in their mouth."

Mike didn't utter a single word until long strands of hot cum shot from Nevin's hard cock, landing like slimy slugs on his exposed belly button. "Fuck, that was nice." Nevin sighed in ecstasy, wiping the cum off his belly with an extra pair of boxers from the back seat.

"I don't want to go to this weird 'get together', Nevin. I almost wish you hadn't asked me to come with you. This shit seems super sketchy. I don't know what has gotten into you lately with this whole *making memories* thing."

Nevin rolled his eyes, tossing the cum covered pair of boxers in the backseat. He was starting to feel the same level of regret that his third-choice date was having, only his regret was the company he decided to keep.

"Well, I guess you shouldn't have come, huh? Maybe you should have reconsidered a few hours ago before we left the fucking city. Not when we're in the middle of fucking nowhere." Nevin stuck the key back in the ignition, looking around to see if any cars were coming. "I can't see shit past these fucking trees."

Mike rolled down the passenger's side window, spitting as far into the ditch beside the car as he could.

"You have a bad taste in your mouth, sweetheart?" Nevin laughed, pulling slowly out of the small, gravel patch that he had parked in.

"I wouldn't have agreed to come if I had known you were going to be such an insensitive fucking douche. If I'm being honest, I'm surprised you asked me at all, considering how much you've been avoiding me lately." Mike huffed, putting his bare feet up on the dash. "Who decides to drive hours away to meet a group of people they met online? I mean, it's 2009. Don't we as a species know better by now?"

Nevin wanted so badly to kick Mike out of the car, leaving him stranded in the middle of nowhere. But knowing that he would be responsible if something happened to Mike inside the car, he decided to keep his foot on the gas pedal, and off the side of Mike's head.

"Exactly, dick fuck! Like you said, it's 2009. People like me aren't easily fooled by some fake Myspace profile. I *know* these people are legit. And who cares how fucking sketchy it seems? I want to do crazy shit that other people never dream of. I don't want to be an old man wishing that he had done something more."

Nevin pointed a stern finger at the side of Mike's face. Mike swatted the finger away, giving Nevin a disgusted side-eye.

"You said they were some kind of weird commune living on a pig farm in the middle of the woods. How much could they possibly know about social media anyways? I bet we're going to end up hanging by our ankles in some creepy fucking basement, all because you're not mentally mature enough to handle the internet." Now, it was Mike's turn to stick his finger in Nevin's face.

"Now, what is it exactly that made you want to drive all the way out here to meet these people, besides you wanting to *'live life on the fucking edge*?' Mike asked curiously, using his pointer finger to scratch the tip of his sunburnt nose.

Mike looked like the average twink. He was tall, skinny, blonde tips, tight jeans, and a striped tank top. He seemed self-conscious about his age, pushing thirty-five might as well be the backside of fifty in his mind.

Nevin was much younger, just shy of twenty-three. No matter how much Nevin pissed him off, Mike felt some sort of strange obligation to keep an eye on him. He once caught Nevin trying to leave the bar with some big ass leather daddy. He had to grab Nevin by the arm and run before he ended up on the back of the big man's motorcycle.

"I don't need you looking out for me, Mike! You're not my daddy, and certainly not my boyfriend! Mind your own business." Nevin would shout in Mike's face every time that he felt Mike being overly protective. Mike only held out hope that once Nevin matured a little, he would settle down.

"You know how I watch those videos online, the ones about the spree-killers?" Mike looked over at Nevin, a sickly feeling starting to build in his stomach.

"Yeah, the ones about Paul Homolka and that kid from a few years back who tried to imitate him. What about em'?"

Mike tried to think of what Nevin was going to say before he said it. He thought back to the time he walked in on Nevin watching those videos on his computer. Mike remembered Nevin's bloodshot eyes, his messy hair from not showering, the pile of empty soda cans piled next to his feet.

"This trip has something to do with *that* shit?" Mike asked, taking a deep breath, checking the mirror for any newly forming pimples on his chin.

"The farm we are going to is the place where Paul Homolka Killed four people, including his foster sister and his
girlfriend, Franny."

Paul Homolka's name sent a chill down Mike's spine. He
remembered seeing all the stuff on the news during Paul
Homolka's killing spree when he was a kid. The supermarket, his foster parent's house, Franny's house, the fucking elementary school crosswalk, even the pig farm where
Nevin was taking him. Why in the hell would someone like
Nevin want to go to a place like that? Nevin was always a
preppy, pretty boy. He was never into this *weird* shit.

"Why would you want to go to that place, Nevin? Do you
even realize all the pain and suffering that Paul Homolka
caused? All the lives he selfishly ruined for no rhyme or
reason. That farm should be burned to the ground, not
populated by a group of serial killer obsessed weirdos who
probably just use the place to squat at." Mike felt the need
to look after Nevin once again, even knowing he would
have his head bitten off for it.

"Are you my fucking keeper, Mike? Are you my fucking
daddy? Is there a goddamn ring on my finger, huh? No, no
there isn't. So please, shut the fuck up and let me make my
own decisions. If I want to do something in my life, I can

fucking do it! Don't act like my fucking parents, always telling me how to think! I'm a fucking adult, and I can do whatever in the fuck I want!" Nevin slapped the steering wheel in frustration.

Mike felt the urge to cry but held it back. "Okay, fine. What is the plan when we get there? Did these people promise you a tour of the place? Are they going to put on a fucking reenactment? What are we going to do here, Nevin?"

Nevin smiled to himself, then cleared his throat loudly. "I'm glad you asked." He patted Mike on the leg, then adjusted the rearview mirror. "The people on the Myspace page told me that they knew where Paul Homolka was. They told me that they could show me where his body is. Hell, maybe they can show me some *more* crazy shit."

Mike nearly fainted in his seat. He used both hands to shake his own head. He turned as far in the passenger's seat as he could, unbuckling his seat belt to make it easier.

"Nevin, I know you've found this new and exciting interest in your life, and for that, I'm happy. But look, going to see the body of the most notorious spree-killer in American history all because some weird chicks on Myspace said they knew where to find it? That shit doesn't sit right with me, and it shouldn't sit right with you either. These people are probably lying to you. How do *they* know where the body is when the fucking FBI couldn't even find it? Think about it for a minute. These people are luring you in so that they can do something terrible to you. And chances are, this isn't the first time that they've done it. But what am I even going on about? You would probably enjoy being tied up and tortured, all so you can have something to talk to your *real* friends about."

Nevin didn't turn to look at Mike, not even a momentary glance. The car was silent for a few moments. Only the sound of the passing breeze as the car flew down the country road.

"You can sit in the car while I go in." Nevin finally spoke up. His tone was stern. Mike knew that he pushed him too far, he acted too much like a parental figure. "You can sit in the car with your cell phone and you can call the police if the fucking aliens come down and abduct me."

Mike pulled his cell from his pocket, flipping it open to see that he had zero service this far out. He glanced over at Nevin, wondering if he should point out that they had no signal to call for help even if they needed to, but he figured it was no use.

"The map says we need to take a left after the sign for Glenn Rock Road," Nevin said, flipping open the map he had printed out earlier that morning.

Mike looked out the window. He hadn't seen a house, or even another car in over two hours. "The man knew how to stay hidden when he wanted to." Mike glanced over at Nevin who was mumbling to himself.

"That kid, Travis something, back in 2001 or 2002, he was obsessed with Paul Homolka. Look where he ended up." Mike said to himself, hoping deep down that Nevin was listening, hanging on his every word.

"Okay, there's the sign for Glenn Rock Road! And by the way, for your information, this isn't *just* about Paul Homolka, it's about the chance to experience something." Nevin pulled the steering wheel hard to the left. The tires screeched loudly.

"What the hell are you trying to do, kill us?" Mike shouted, slapping his hand down on the center console.

Nevin paid him no attention, his eyes fixated on the gravel road they were now driving down. "I don't think this road was made for cars, it's too fucking narrow, Nevin."

Nevin continued to ignore Mike, who was now becoming increasingly frustrated. "Are you *fucking* listening to me, Nevin? Do you fucking hear what I am saying to you?" Mike leaned over and tapped on the horn.

Nevin slammed on the brakes, causing the red Ford Focus to slide a few feet before coming to a complete stop. As soon as the dust settled, Mike noticed a large, makeshift sign ahead of them.

'Road Closed No Trespassing'

Mike found it difficult to swallow after looking over to see the grin on Nevin's face. Even at a time like this, it was impossible to not notice how beautiful Nevin was.

"He's like a Greek statue come to life." Mike once told his mother on the phone as he smiled in the bathroom mirror.

"It looks like I'm going to have to walk the rest of the way. There is supposed to be an old cabin in the clearing, then the farm is about half a mile south of it." Nevin looked at the handwritten directions on the back of the map. Mike found it had to believe that someone like Nevin could be so goddamn foolish, so fucking gullible.

"Nevin, I'm telling you; this doesn't seem like a good idea."

Nevin sighed loudly, not even taking the time to tell Mike to go and fuck himself. He reached in the backseat, grabbing the large maroon colored bag that he kept his football equipment in during high school. Mike begged Nevin time and time again to throw the damned thing away and to quit putting clean clothes in it. But like most things out of Mike's mouth, they were quickly dismissed with the wave of a hand. Right before Nevin could open his door, Mike grabbed his arm so tightly that he cried out in pain.

"What in the fuck are you doing? Are you fucking nuts? Let go of my arm!"

Mike didn't say a word, he just pointed towards the driver's side window, his face now ghostly white.

"Who are they?" Mike's voice cracked, a tear now running down the side of his cheek.

Nevin turned his head slowly, locking eyes with the two young women who were just inches from his window.

"Nevin, we need to go."

Mike's entire body was now shaking. He had never been so scared in his life. The two girls couldn't be any older than eighteen or nineteen. Both of them had long, straight brown hair that hung down past their shoulders, their face's both soft, pale, and expressionless.

"Are you Nevin?" the girl on the right asked, touching her thin, frail hand to the glass.

Nevin glanced over at Mike, then back at the girls. "Um, yeah, I'm Nevin. Is one of you Farmgirl1990?"

Mike nearly croaked when he heard the username that these strange people had been using.

"What in the fuck kind of name is that? These people are fucking weird, Nevin. Put the car in reverse and let's get the hell out of here!" The girl on the left looked up at Mike, a stern and disapproving look made his blood run cold.

"You never told us that you were bringing a friend along," the girl on the left whispered, moving her pale face closer to the glass. Her breath fogged up a spot on the window, she rubbed her pointer finger over it, making a tiny smiley face.

"You should follow us up to the farm. Everyone is waiting for you." The girl on the right added, taking a step back to allow Nevin to open his door.

"No! Fuck this shit! We need to get the hell out of here, Nevin! These people are fucking weird!" Mike reached over to grab the keys from Nevin's hand, but he quickly jerked away. "This isn't some kind of fucking game, Nevin! These people are fucking strange. Can't you see that?"

Nevin reached down, pulling the handle to open the driver's side door.

"You can sit here, or you can come with me. Your choice. But you will not ruin this for me, understand? Keep your fucking mouth shut and let me enjoy this, okay?"

Strangely, Mike felt bad when he saw the sad look in Nevin's eyes. This was fucking weird, and Mike knew that, but he couldn't bring himself to upset Nevin any further. If there was ever any hope for a future between the two of them, he knew he needed to start trusting Nevin. Even if his ideas were batshit crazy.

"I'll come with you, Nevin." Mike forced a smile as he put the palm of his hand on Nevin's cheek. Nevin smiled back at him for the first time in months. "Just promise me that if we make it out of here alive, you'll let me move in with you." The two of them laughed together, then kissed before stepping out of the car.

"Just follow us, we'll show you exactly what you wanted to see." The girl on the right said with a smile, motioning for the two men to follow.

Mike looked concerningly at Nevin before following the girls up a steep hillside and into a large open field. It was slowly driving Mike mad that the two girls weren't wearing any shoes, only long white gowns.

"The look like they're a part of some weird fucking cult," Mike whispered in Nevin's ear as they followed closely behind the two girls. "Who in the fuck walks around in the woods without shoes, and in fucking nightgowns? Do you find that just a tad fucking odd, or am I the only *'sane one'* in the group?"

Nevin shrugged his shoulders, his eyes darting from left to right as they continued through the large open field.

"Holy fuck!" Nevin gasped, placing his hand on Mike's chest to stop him from continuing. "Look!" Nevin pointed straight ahead, his eyes the size of dinner plates, his mouth hanging down like a cartoon dog seeing a pretty woman in a tight red dress.

Mike looked ahead in the direction that Nevin was pointing, a tiny old cabin sat in the center of the field, tall grass grown up around it, the windows shattered, the front door boarded up with a sheet of plywood. "It's the cabin where Paul hid out for over a fucking decade!" The level of excitement in Nevin's voice was concerning, but Mike was glad to see him this happy.

"That's really great man, really great." Mike looked over at the two girls who stood about eight or nine feet away holding hands, giggling as they whispered in each other's ears. For some reason, this annoyed Mike. He wondered if this was set up to look creepy, like some fucked up, macabre murder tour. He wondered if Nevin gave these people money for this little outing.

"How much money did you give these crazy ass people? It wasn't a lot, was it? I know you were saving up for that condo. You didn't give them any of your personal information, did you?"

Nevin couldn't take his eyes away from the old cabin, his heart raced so quickly that he had to take a deep breath before responding to Mike.

"Money?" Was the only thing Nevin blurted out as he finally took his attention off the cabin. Mike looked back once more at the girls. They continued to smile in his and Nevin's direction, giggling to one another quietly.

"How much did my *idiot* friend here pay you for this fucked up little tour?" Mike asked defensively. The girls started giggling again, whispering in one another's ears. "What's with the whispering? Is there some kind of inside joke that he and I aren't privy to? If so, spit it the fuck out and say it where I can fucking hear it!" Mike took a step forward, biting down on his bottom lip.

The girls stopped smiling, blank, emotionless expressions burying their once creepy grins.

"Your friend didn't pay us a thing because we didn't ask for his money. NevDaddy441 contacted us through Myspace, asking about the farm in our pictures." The girl on the right looked over her shoulder towards an opening in the trees. "He said that he had seen it in a documentary, asked if he could come out to see it in person."

Mike looked back at Nevin. He nodded his head.

"You two live on that pig farm, the one where those murders took place?" Mike asked, feeling uneasy once again.

The two girls nodded, then smiled. "It's not *just* the two of us. We have some other family there as well." Now that uneasy feeling had quickly turned into a swirling, tumor-like mass of fear. "Your friend seemed so eager; we just couldn't find it in our hearts to say no." The girl on the left turned to the girl on the right, running her pointer finger across her thin, red lips. "We told him he could come and stay with us for as long as he wanted, just as long as he brought us something in return." It felt as if someone had dropped an ice cube straight from the freezer down the back of Mike's shirt.

"You act like such a good friend, Mike. It's really hard to believe he chose to bring someone like you. I mean, the last person that we invited brought along her stepfather, she hated him more than anything in the world. But, for our new friend, Nevin, to bring someone as caring as *you*? It's a real shame. Something hard and heavy cracked Mike in the back of the head, knocking him out cold.

Chapter Two

LOLLIPOPS AND CHAINSAWS

"It's been two fucking years, Paul! You couldn't give her a few more years to grow the fuck up before you started sniffing her dirty underwear?" Franny never shouted at me; she knew better. Now, normally I would bust her fucking head open, then help her to keep her mouth occupied. But I needed to be chill, I needed the violent predator inside of me to take a long fucking nap until I felt it was time to move on. We had been couped-up in this fucking cabin for two years, it was starting to drive the three of us a little mad. I looked out the window at Mary-Ann, she was building a really shitty looking snowman right out front.

"I wasn't 'sniffing' her underwear. I was wiping my nose. Not my fault that her underwear was the closest thing." I snapped, pulling out the small wooden chair from under the kitchen table. "I have that prick cop still up my ass, and no one is forgetting about the fucking grocery store incident anytime soon. So, I need you to take a fucking breath, and shut the fuck up." I almost slammed my fist down on the table but stopped myself.

"This just isn't the life that I pictured for us when we met, that's all." Franny looked out the window at Mary-Ann, her eyes empty, devoid of all emotion. I laughed for the first time in what felt like ages.

"You mean after I made you eat your dead stepdaddy's ass? After we killed your trailer park whore of a mother? This isn't the life you expected after all that? Fuck, you're so much fucking stupider than I thought." I continued laughing as the emotionless look in Franny's eyes grew like fresh blood on a white T-shirt.

"I never signed on to be that girl's mother, Paul."

My laughter turned to a growl as I lunged forward across the tiny wooden table. I grabbed Franny by the hair, yanking her up out of her seat.

"You'll be whatever the fuck I want you to be, understand?" I slapped Franny in the face as hard as I could, still holding tightly to her long, greasy hair. "I pulled you out of that fucking shithole, you fucking owe me everything you have, and every fucking thing you'll ever get!" I closed my fist, cracking Franny in the jaw over and over again until her body went limp. "You worthless fucking whore! You dreamed of sunshine and rainbows for far too long, you dumb cunt."

I let her unconscious body drop to the cabin floor. "I need to be at fucking peace in this place if I'm ever going to have a chance to reenter the normal world, a more vicious killer than I was before!" I kicked Franny in the ribs as hard as I could before lying down on the couch for a nap.

Over the years, Franny grew more and more absent, her mind constantly wandering, eventually growing far too comfortable with our time spent in the cabin. Something had changed in her; I could sense it.

"Why do you keep touching your fucking stomach?" I asked one night after tossing a few logs in the fireplace. Franny looked up at me as she ran a brush through Mary-Ann's hair. Mary-Ann rolled her eyes, her teenage years were full of annoying little quirks like that.

"I don't know. I've been throwing up; I can't keep any food down for longer than thirty minutes."

I thought about the rabbit I had killed two nights before, how Franny spat it back out into her bowl.

"To be honest, Paul, I think I might be pregnant."

Mary-Ann and I both locked eyes. She got to her feet and walked to the back bedroom, closing the door quietly behind her. Franny lowered her head, twiddling her thumbs like a complete fucking spaz. I wasn't sure exactly how to react. Maybe I should react the way that Mary-Ann assumed I would, hinting why she put herself as far away from Franny and I as she could without running to the other side of the planet.

This couldn't be happening. Not now, not while life in the cabin was just starting to settle, not just when I started to find some inner fucking peace.

"How can you be pregnant, Fanny? You're a disgusting fuck hole that has been rammed by at least fifty or sixty guys, not counting your grandpa and stepdaddy. How did you manage to keep that cum out of you while your old, saggy grandpa, busted his prehistoric load in that tight young snatch of yours, huh?" Franny shook her head without looking back up at me.

"Did you fish the cum out with your fucking hand? Did your pussy fart it out when you sat down on your stepdads' lap? Tell me, Franny, how in the fuck a little fucking slut like you, could somehow be pregnant all of a sudden?"

Franny continued fiddling with her thumbs, shaking her fucking head like she had some sort of retard twitch. Finally, she raised her head up, her tears seemed to only anger me further.

"I don't know, Paul. It's not like you'd want to keep it anyways, right?"

Thankfully, I laughed. I was so thankful for laughing because at least I knew that I still had my sense of humor intact.

Franny lowered her head again. "We could have a really good life raising a family here."

I stood up from my chair, looking down in disgust on the total fucking moron who sat before me.

"We are living off the fucking grid, you dumb bitch. We get water from a fucking creek that we have to boil in a pot over the fucking fireplace! I have to hunt rabbits like some piece of redneck white trash! What kind of mother would want that kind of life for her child? Do you want your baby to grow up in some little house on the fucking prairie storybook? Is that what you want, Franny."

I heard Mary-Ann trying to hold back laughter in the back bedroom, which, in turn, made *me* laugh for the second time tonight. Franny's face turned red from what I assumed was embarrassment. "It seems like I'm not the only one in this cabin who thinks you sound like a dumb fucking bitch." Mary-Ann finally started cracking up in the other room.

"Well, how about the two of you tell me what in the fuck I should do!" Franny jumped to her feet, kicking the hairbrush that she had brushed Mary-Ann's hair with. "Tell me, Paul. What is it that you want to do?"

I had never actually seen Franny so angry. I will admit, my cock started getting hard.

"I would do anything for you, Paul. You know that, right? So please, tell me what you want me to do. Should I have this fucking kid, if I'm even pregnant? Or should I shove a kitchen knife up my cunt and twist it?"

It was hard to tell if Franny was being sarcastic, it always was with someone as fucking stupid as her.

"Lay on the floor." I whispered with a smile. Something seemed to flicker behind Franny's eyes. "Lay down flat on your back."

I pointed towards the floor. She did exactly as I asked. "Now, take off those fucking pants and start playing with your pussy, get it wet for me." Once again, Franny did as I asked. Before I walked into the kitchen, I noticed how thick her cunt bush was getting. It made me want to fucking vomit.

I heard Franny moaning as I rummaged through one of the drawers in the tiny kitchen. "Bingo." I smiled at my reflection in the menacingly sharp blade of a filet knife. When I re-entered the room, Franny was moaning loudly, seemingly on the verge of an orgasm. I dropped down to my knees, pulling my hard cock from my pants. I wondered if Mary-Ann had learned how to play with her pussy yet.

"Suck my cock while you use this inside your worn-out dick tunnel." Franny's eyes grew large, I knew it was fear.

"Paul, that is really going to fuck me up." Her bottom lip quivered as another tear rolled down her face and onto the floor underneath her head.

I put my thumb in her mouth, pushing it as far down as I could get it. She gagged, slapping and clawing at my arm as she tried to break free.

"I don't give a fuck what it does to your nasty fucking hole, you hear me? I told you to stick the motherfucker in, now fucking do it before I ram my entire fist down your fucking throat." I handed Franny the knife, knowing damn well she wasn't stupid enough to try using it on me. "Use it like you would a rotted cock, go in and out really slow at first, then go to fucking town with it, work out that arm a little."

Franny gagged louder and cried harder. "I won't- I won't be-"

I took my finger out of Franny's mouth so that she could better articulate. "I won't be able to cum using this." Franny took at look at the knife in her hand.

"I don't want you to come, Sweetheart. I want you to bleed."

CHAPTER THREE

THE GIRLS AND THEIR PETS

MIKE'S EYES THROBBED. HE had the worst headache he'd ever had in his life. Was that smoke he was smelling? His throat burned like he had just escaped the tenth floor of a burning building. Was it morning? How long had he been out? Did someone hit him on the back of the head with something?

He pushed himself up to see a small campfire sitting in the middle of what appeared to be a large pig pen. He ran his hand softly over the large lump on the back of his head, tiny pieces of dried blood covering his fingertips. Mike turned his head to see an old two-story house sat only a few yards behind where he was lying. *"The pig farm."* A distant voice deep in the back of his mind called out, lost in the fog that clouded his brain.

"Nevin?" Mike called out, trying desperately to pull himself up to his feet. "Nevin?" he called out again, losing his balance due to his left leg being asleep.

The sound of women's laughter could be heard from inside the house, Mike suddenly felt eyes watching his every move. The most insidious of thoughts began to make the hairs on his arms stand up, and his mouth go dry. What if Nevin had been taken by those two girls? What if they had him locked in the basement, torturing him?

"Nevin? Can you hear me?" Mike cupped his hands over his mouth, shouting as loud as he could. "What did you do with my friend?!"

He used his anger to keep himself standing long enough to limp over to the old wooden fence. The girls were too far away to have been the ones to hit him. He tried to collect his thoughts, but it was like a dog trying to piss on the tire of a moving car. Had someone hit Nevin before hitting *him*?

"Pussy!" a woman shouted from somewhere near the farmhouse. Mike couldn't pinpoint where from.

"What did you motherfuckers do with Nevin!?" Mike shouted, pushing open the gate, wanting the hell out of the pig pen he had woken up in. From the corner of his eye, he could have sworn he saw movement from an upstairs window.

"I saw you; I fucking saw you, Bitch! Come down here right the *fuck* now!" Mike slammed the gate closed, rattling the entire fence so badly that a few of the loose boards fell to the ground.

"Oink, Oink, come on piggy, *this* way." Mike turned to see one of the girls standing on the front porch, her pale skin matching the faded, cracked paint on the front door. Mike clenched his fists, the adrenalin giving him the extra kick to run as fast as he could towards the woman who was now laughing at him. "Come on, little piggy!" The woman turned on her heels, disappearing back into the house.

"What the hell am I doing? She's obviously baiting me. How fucking stupid would I be to go in that place?" Mike asked himself out loud, placing his hands on his hips and taking a few deep breaths.

"Mike! Help me!" Nevin's voice called out from the house. As much as Mike didn't want to, his legs began running again towards the front door.

"Nevin, I'm coming, man!" As soon as Mike rammed his shoulder into the wooden door, he braced himself for a large man wearing a skin mask to hit him over the head with a hammer.

"Nevin?" He called out past the crackling of his own voice. "Where are you?"

He waited for a response, but there was nothing to be heard other than the creaking of the floor under his feet. The house smelled of mildew, the way wet cardboard smelled after leaving it out in the rain. The wallpaper looked to be from another time. The light switches had been ripped from the walls, leaving only exposed wires. Mike took a step forward, his foot getting caught on a strand of old police caution tape.

"Oink, Oink, Piggy, Piggy." A woman Mike hadn't seen before was now standing at the top of the stairs. She was dressed almost identically to the two girls from before.

"What did you crazy bitches do with Nevin?" Fear wrapped its hands around Mike's throat, making it harder and harder to breathe. The girl smiled, then gave him a wink before disappearing around the corner.

"Wait!"

Mike took a step towards the stairs, wondering what would be waiting for him once he reached the top. The doubt he'd felt outside had started making him question his decisions. He had seen far too many horror movies; he knew he was making the most classic of mistakes. "I would be screaming for me to turn around and make a run for it if this were a movie I was watching on tv."

Mike quickly turned around, making a run for the front door. He didn't even bother running down the three or four steps on the porch. He hopped over the railing like he'd seen someone do on an episode of Cops.

"Your friend is smarted than *you* gave him credit for." Luna said as she turned from the upstairs window to look at Nevin, who was tied to a chair in the middle of the room. Her two sisters, Venus and Pluto, looked at each other confusingly.

"What do we do now?" asked Pluto, gripping tightly on the barbed wire wrapped baseball bat in her hands. Luna turned back to the window to see Mike running through the opening in the woods towards the field where the old cabin sat. Luna smiled to herself, imagining Mike looking for the car that would no longer be there.

"He won't make it far. Jupiter is out hunting; she'll make sure our new friend is back here before lunch."

Nevin jumped at the sound of multiple babies crying in unison from a room across the hall. Luna nodded at Venus, signaling her to go and tend to the children, Venus sighed loudly, dropping the Axe she was holding on a table by the door.

"You said if I brought someone I didn't care for, you would take them and let me be a part of this." Nevin spit blood from his mouth, feeling the spot where two of his teeth were knocked out a few hours prior.

Luna turned to Nevin, her white silk gown dancing at her ankles. A handmade crown of dead flowers rested atop her black, greasy hair.

"And I was telling the truth, you are going to be a part of this. We just can't have you trying to run off like your friend once you find out the part you're going to play."

Nevin shook his head, his neck tender from a fall he had taken down the steps. "I don't care what part I play; I swear it! I want this! Just tell me what to do!"

Luna and Pluto smiled at one another, almost as if they were hearing an inside joke that only the two of them could understand.

Nevin became frustrated, pulling at the chains that held his hands in place, and the chair to the floor. "I wouldn't have agreed to come if I wasn't fucking serious! What do I have to do to prove myself?" Nevin pleaded, leaning towards Luna as far as he could. "I want to know more about Paul Homolka. You said you knew where to find him. Does my part have anything to do with what happened here with Mary-Ann or Franny?"

Strangely, Luna rubbed her stomach softly, like an expectant mother. "We were here long before Paul, Franny, And Mary-Ann ever found that old cabin to hide out in. We were actually kept in chains out in the barn when Paul was held captive in the basement. My sisters and I lived very troubled lives when our fathers were still alive. Thankfully, Paul came along and took care of them, stopping the family reunions that our fathers would throw, always resulting in more sisters for us to care for."

Nevin felt sick to his stomach, now realizing why these girls were all so fucking strange. "You're- um, you're all sisters?"

He felt Pluto step closer to him, so close he could feel her hot breath on the back of his neck. "So, what do you need me to do?" he asked, quickly trying to backtrack, hoping he hadn't already dug his grave.

Luna smiled up at Pluto before reaching her hand out towards her sister.

"Can I ask where all those babies in the other room came from?"

Luna lowered her outstretched arm, then used her pointer finger to wipe some of the blood and sweat from Nevin's forehead. "Those babies were given to us by someone really special, someone we keep just to ourselves."

Nevin didn't quite understand what in the hell Luna was talking about. Whatever it was, he was sure it was something as batshit crazy as she herself. "The part we need you to play, Nevin, is the part of giving my sisters your very special seed." Luna squatted down, resting her elbows on Nevin's knees. "Our current doner is quite special, but is becoming very reluctant to give us what we ask for." Luna rubbed her filthy hands over the bulge in Nevin's shorts.

"You want me to be some kind of sex slave to you and your sisters?" He looked at Luna, then up at Pluto, his eyes wide with surprise.

Pluto nodded at him, placing her hand on his shoulder before leaning forward to sniff his hair. "My sisters and I chose *you* over your friend because you still look so young, so fertile. If I'm being honest, we're really glad that you gave us options. It would have been quite a shame if you had brought a woman with you. We would've killed her rather quickly. Mars and Celeste were responsible for choosing between you and your friend, I feel they made the right decision."

Nevin thought about the two girls who met him and Mike at the car when they arrived.

"We hope that you're able to accommodate all of our needs."

He wondered how many of these inbred sisters were running around the area, watching from the trees. Luna pushed herself up using Nevin's legs, then slowly reached down to grab the bottom of her white gown. She lifted it above her belly button, revealing a thick bush, and a smell that made Nevin gag.

"Celeste was worried that you may be attracted to other men like yourself. That's not the case, is it?"

It felt as if a boulder had dropped onto Nevin's chest, knocking all the air from his lungs.

"Of course not! I like pussy. That's all I've ever liked." He felt his cheeks glowing red, hoping like hell that Pluto didn't notice. "Why do you all want so many kids? Is this some kind of cult or something?" Nevin wondered if he'd regret asking such a forward question but was quickly relieved when Luna began laughing hysterically.

"I wouldn't say that, not exactly. I'd say that we're just a big, happy family that only wants to grow and survive like any other."

"Sounds like a fucking cult to me." Nevin fought to keep himself from saying out loud.

"We want our family to be big and strong, that's why we want strong men like yourself to help us. We've had a few boys slip through the cracks, but we take care of them the second they take their first breaths." Luna nodded to Pluto, who danced slowly over to the closet on the far-left side of the room. She pulled the door open, resulting in

Nevin being unable to keep himself from vomiting any longer.

"What in the fuck! What in the fuck! What in the fuck!" Nevin screamed, rocking back and forth in his chair, trying to keep his eyes shut. An arm wrapped around his neck, locking him in a tight headlock. Venus had re-entered the room.

"Shut the fuck up! If you wake the children, I'll rip your fucking heart out!" Venus growled her warning in Nevin's ear before licking the side of his face like an eager house dog. "Open your eyes and look! Look at what happens to the boys who aren't welcome here!" Venus used her free hand to pry open Nevin's eyes. "Look at them and make goddamn sure that *you* stay useful."

Nevin couldn't help but look at the absolute horror before him. There had to be at least twenty-five newborn babies covering the closet wall, each of them with large, rusty nails driven into the front of their head. Some of the tiny bodies had already become skeletons, some were in advanced stages of decomposition, their brown flesh dripping down onto the floor in large puddles.

"Please, please close the door! I understand, I promise, I understand!"

Pluto smiled before kicking the closet door shut with the bottom of her foot.

A loud whistle from outside caused Luna to drop her gown and run over to the window. "Looks like your friend didn't make it very far." Luna waved at the two sisters dragging the bloody and beaten man behind them with chains as he fought to get free.

Chapter Four

Hog Tied and Fucked Soft

I HAD STARTED TO lose track of how many years we had been hidden away in this fucking cabin. I noticed how nice and round Mary-Ann's little tits were getting, so it must have been six years or so by this point. Franny continued teaching the growing girl how to do math and read. I wish she had been teaching her how to please me. But at least I wouldn't have to lug around a fucking retard when we finally left this place.

I knew I was fucking insane; I knew there was something not right about me; I fucking knew I wanted to feel my knife cut through the flesh of another human being again. But as much as I wanted it, I knew I had to be patient. Patience was always one of my best attributes alongside rape and murder. I could have left this place already, I could have crept in Mary-Ann's bedroom and raped the shit out of her, but it was all about patience. I would get out of here one day, and I would certainly have my hard cock in Mary-Ann's virgin pussy. For now, I just sat my fucking ass on the fort porch of the cabin staring through the trees at the pig farm that sat about a hundred and fifty yards through the tree line. I had never been worried about the two inbred looking fucks that inhabited that shithole. Every once and awhile you could hear human, female screams over the sound of the hogs kept in a pen out front. These fuckers didn't want the extra attention.

"Paul?" I turned to Mary-Ann, who had snuck up on me without my noticing. She had her arms crossed, looking like a young teenage girl from the movies I used to watch at the numerous foster homes. Fuck, I couldn't wait to destroy her.

"Yeah, what is it? Franny yapping your fucking head off again?" I laughed, spitting a big loogi over the porch railing.

Franny looked out into the trees for a few seconds before sitting beside me on the porch swing. "What do I have to do to get you to let me leave? I want out of here, Paul. I want to go and live the life that a teenage girl like me should be living. I want my license, I want a boyfriend, hell, I want any type of friend at this point. And please do me a favor, don't give me any shit about us being in hiding. Out of the three of us, I would be the least noticeable, considering I'm no longer a little girl in pigtails."

I had already heard this exact shit from Mary-Ann before, it seemed to change slightly the older she got. I wondered how much of it was spoon-fed to her by Franny, I wouldn't put it past the crazy bitch to plant such thoughts in Mary-Ann's head. Franny wanted me all to herself, I had known that since the day I told her that Mary-Ann was coming along for the ride. Here Franny was thinking this was going to be some kind of Bonnie and Clyde love story. Little did she know, Clyde didn't give a flying fuck about Bonnie.

"Mary-Ann, we've had this talk how many times now? It always goes the same fucking way. What makes this time any different than the last?"

She was quick to respond, like she already knew what I was going to say before I said it.

"I'm older now, Paul. I'm not a little girl anymore. Don't you see that?" She stood up from the swing to show me how big she had gotten. "I can't waste anymore of my life here, Paul, I just can't. I want to go out and start my life, live the childhood that I missed out on because of you. Why in the fuck would you want *this* life for me?" She bit her bottom lip to keep herself from saying anymore.

"Where would you go, Mary-Ann? Huh? Where in the fuck would you go? Did you plan on hiking out of here until you got to the main road, only to stick your thumb out and wait for some fucking creep to pick up the hot young piece of ass on the side of the road? Have you thought about it, huh? Have you really fucking thought it though? Even if some old creep doesn't rape and dismember you, what are you going to do once you make it back to civilization? Are you going to and go back to school? Are you going to work at some shitty burger place to pay for some shithole apartment you rented from some fat maggot piece of trash?" I felt my neck getting hot and my palms start to itch.

"The world isn't the fucking cesspool that you make it out to be, Paul! Not everyone out there is some worthless fucking maggot that only deserves to die! I don't know where in the fuck you picked up that idea. You and I lived in all the same places and knew all the same people. Why didn't I turn out like you? Why don't I hate the fucking world, Paul?"

The conversation had never gotten this fucking far before. I always just told Mary-Ann to shut the fuck up and piss off. She would stomp her feet and run inside to her room crying until she got the fuck over it. It was painfully clear that this time was going to be a much bigger pain in my fucking ass.

"Look, Mary-Ann, you fucking-"

"Hello over there!"

Mary-Ann and I both turned to see some fucking dude in a bright yellow jacket wearing a backpack and carrying a walking stick. It was the first time Mary-Ann had seen another man besides me in years. "I hope I'm not trespassing, or worse, interrupting an important conversation." The man laughed awkwardly as he looked around the open field. "I have to be honest, I'm a little lost. I was supposed to be near *'Glenn something road'* about two hours ago. I found this clearing and decided to see if I could spot the highway from it."

I rolled my eyes, then pulled myself to my feet. "I don't really need your life story, buddy." I smiled, hoping the little fish would bite my big shiny hook so that I could reel him in quickly before he swam away. This was the exact shit I had spent years worrying about, some do-gooder fucking faggot with a backpack coming up to the front porch.

"Get him to come up here. I might just consider what we were talking about." I whispered to Mary-Ann without being too obvious about doing so.

"What's your name?" Mary-Ann asked with a flirtatious smile, waving her hand in the air like the motherfucker hadn't already been eyeballing her the entire time.

The hiker smiled back, feeling comfortable enough to take a few steps closer towards us. "The name's Jasper. What might yours be?"

I turned my head and rolled my eyes. What a fucking dildo this guy was. I noticed that he looked much younger than he had from far away. I'd guess eighteen or nineteen at the most. A few things were certain about our new guest. One, he was very interested in Mary-Ann. Two, he was very naive and stupid. And third, he was going to die a very violent death.

"I'm Mary-Ann. You must be super tired from all that hiking. Why don't you come up and have a seat?" She waved the boy over. He took a few more steps before the two of us locked eyes. It reminded me of a deer seeing the eyes of a wolf in the brush.

"Are *you,* her father?" Jasper asked, looking away from me as he asked the question.

I laughed, placing my hand on Mary-Ann's shoulder. "Something like that." I smiled, running my fingers down Mary-Ann's arm. I wondered if Jasper noticed.

The chills on Mary-Ann's soft flesh made my cock hard. I wondered if our new friend noticed *that* as well. He cleared his throat before taking a few more steps toward the front porch. I bet his mommy and daddy taught him not to talk to strangers. I mean, shit, how were you ever supposed to meet new people?

From the corner of my eye, I spotted the raggy old curtains moving. Franny peered through the window, my 1911 pistol held with both hands up to her chest. I could tell she was waiting for some sort of signal. I didn't want to draw too much attention towards Franny and end up spooking Jasper.

"So, why are you out here hiking all alone? You don't have any friends to go hiking with?" Mary-Ann asked, slowly twisting her pointer finger in her hair. Jasper cleared his throat again, looking up at me to see if I had noticed his eyes scanning every inch of her tight little body.

"I- um- I just figured it would be more of a challenge to do it alone. I like to live on the edge as much as I can, you know?" He smiled, pulling his backpack further up on his shoulders. This little prick thought he was impressing my little sister; thought he was going to swoop her off her feet with his perfectly white teeth and his boyish good looks. Little did Jasper the cocksucker know, Mary-Ann was smarter than he was.

"Wow, you must be super brave! I wish I was brave enough to do something as crazy as hiking a trial all by myself." Jasper's face turned so red that if I had just walked out the door and saw him standing there, I would think he was choking on his chewing gum.

"Yeah- I mean, no. Um, so do you guys have a phone I can use, and maybe some water to drink? I'd really like to call my mom and let her know that I'm doing alright." I shrugged my shoulders, giving Jasper my best impression of an inviting smile.

"Sure thing, Kid, come on in and use the phone in the kitchen."

Jasper looked up at the roof, and then around the wide-open field. I smirked, knowing I was wrong about the kid being so fucking stupid. He turned to look behind him, then turned back to Mary-Ann and I concerningly.

"No telephone lines." I said under my breath, just low enough that Mary-Ann could hear.

"Um, I guess you guys are pretty off the grid all the way out here."

It was now Mary-Ann's turn to reel in the fish.

"My mother inside the cabin has a portable phone, the reception isn't all that great, but you should be able to at least reach out to your mom to let her know that you're safe."

Jasper turned to look behind him once more, then positioned his backpack further up on his shoulders.

"I really appreciate it, but I think I'm going to take that trail and see where it leads. I'm always up for a new challenge." He chuckled awkwardly before slowly backing away from Mary-Ann and I. "Good luck with living off the grid, I wish you all well."

Before Jasper could turn his back, I was already off the porch and running towards him. You want to know what my favorite thing is about killing? It's not the shooting, it's not the stabbing, it's not even the dismembering of a body. For me, it was the look in their eyes. It was a very distinctive look, one that was impossible to fake. It was the look on their faces when they knew that they were absolutely fucked.

"Little fucking maggots like you make me fucking sick!" It had been so long since I had taken a human life, so I would take my time taking Jaspers.

"Please! Sir! I didn't do anything!"

I grabbed ahold of Jasper's backpack, slinging him to the ground as hard as I could. He was a big boy and would have made a worthy adversary if not for the fact that instead of leaning to fight in his free time, he hiked like some pussy ass faggot. I stomped down hard on his back with my heel, feeling his spine bend under the meat.

He screamed, causing Franny to rush out onto the porch next to Mary-Ann. I placed my foot on the flat of Jaspers back, then grabbed him by the shoulders.

CRACK!

There was a thunderous pop as I pulled back his shoulders. The familiar smell of shit creeped up my nose. This fucking kid screamed louder than anyone I had ever heard.

"I had never thought about pulling back on the shoulders, you know?" I looked up at Franny and Mary-Ann. Franny smiled, like a light switch had been flipped on in her empty head.

Mary-Ann scoffed at me, rolling her eyes as she walked up the porch and into the cabin. I winked at Franny as I grabbed Jasper by the ankle, dragging him towards the little woodshed.

I let Franny eat the shit out of jasper's ass crack, something she was a fucking pro at. She smiled at me like a fat kid who just face fucked a Dutch chocolate cake.

I used a pair of pliers to rip Jasper's front teeth out so that he couldn't bite my cock when I rammed it in his mouth. "You week little fucks always make me cum, fucking always." I grabbed Jasper's ears, using them to pull his head up and down. I knew he would vomit; I just didn't realize how much.

"Looks like he's surviving on oatmeal or something. Must be all that gay ass hiking food." I pulled Jasper's head off my cock. "Do you eat any *real* food, Jasper?"

Franny laughed as more blood and bile oozed from my new fuck-hole. She crawled across the shed floor, her perky tits dangling like a fucking pregnant goat.

"Did you save some cum for me?" She asked, grabbing my limp, bloody cock in her hand. I laughed, pushing her away.

"You want my cum? Get it out of his stomach." I chuckled, wiping my cock off with her dirty panties. I thought about snapping Jasper's neck but decided to just leave him in the shed to die on his own.

"I think Mary-Ann hates me." I sighed, leaning up against the shed door as Jasper cried out for help.

"Yeah? What's new?" Franny asked, shrugging her shoulders as she slipped her nasty underwear back on.

Chapter Five

REBIRTH OF A SIREN WHORE

Gasoline burned Mike's eyes as he was forced from his unconscious slumber. "Wha- What the fuck!" Mike gasped for breath, taking in small sips of gas that dripped down his lips and nose. He looked around at the group of scary looking women in white gowns that surrounded him. "Who the fuck are you crazy bitches?! Huh?! Who the fuck are you and what are you doing to me!?"

He was tied up to an old flagpole a few yards from the pig pen he had woken up in the first time. "I knew from the get-go that you fucking cunts were crazy, I fucking knew it! Where is Nevin? What have you freaks done with my friend?" Mike looked around in every direction that he could, hoping to see Nevin still alive.

"Maybe he's the strong one." Pluto whispered to Luna, looking Mike up and down.

Luna tilted her head to the left, wondering if her sister noticed something that she herself hadn't. "Your friend. He volunteered to stay here with us. He no longer needs you."

Mike glared confusingly at Luna, then around at the rest of the girls that circled him. "Volunteered? What in the hell are you talking about? Nevin can be pretty fucking naive, but he would never agree to shit like this!"

The strange group of girls giggled like they knew something that Mike didn't.

"Why in the fuck are you laughing? If you have something to say before you fucking kill me, say it!"

Luna turned, pointing a finger towards the old barn Nevin was now making his way from. Even from as far away as he was, Mike could see the disturbed look on Nevin's pretty, young face. It was a look as if someone had just yanked the soul from his body, leaving just a husk that would wander around, lost to the world.

"Nevin! Tell me that you have no idea what's going on here! Tell me this is some kind of sick fucking joke!"

Nevin made his way next to Luna and Pluto, his hands deep in his pockets, his head lowered to the ground.

"Nevin! Fucking answer, me!" Mike's voice started to shake, he tried to hide the tears running down his blood-red-cheeks.

"Venus." Luna nodded to her sister. Venus nodded back, lifting a 4-foot-long two-by-four with rusted circle saw blades crudely driven into the end. "You'll watch until the end. If you even blink, I'll have one of my sisters cut your legs off so we can watch you crawl until you bleed to death."

Luna grabbed a handful of Nevin's hair, jerking his head up so that he had to watch what was about to happen to his friend. Venus swung downwards with the piece of wood, one of the blades catching Mike on the side of his face. Mike screamed as the rusted blade was yanked out.

"Nevin!" Mike cried, the two-by-four cracking him on the top of the head.

Nevin had nothing left to vomit. He just stood there, dry heaving as his friend was beaten almost to death. By the time Venus dropped her handmade weapon to the ground, Mike was unrecognizable, but still alive. Luna pulled Nevin's hair once more, making sure he witnessed the destruction her sister had caused. Chunks of cartilage and flesh dangled from Mike's nose, thick, long gashes were deep enough that you could see parts of his skull. The breaking point was seeing Mike's bottom lip resting on his bloody shirt like a dead slug.

"Finish him."

Nevin looked up into Luna's cold grey eyes. The sebum on her nose and chin looked like sweat in the sunlight. If Luna had been a close friend, maybe even a next-door neighbor, Nevin would offer her a facewipe containing zero alcohol. Hell, maybe even a decent shampoo and conditioner combo to add some life to her flat, greasy hair.

"Why do I have to kill him?" Nevin asked through his dry, chapped lips. He still didn't quite understand what in the hell drove these crazy women to do the things that they did. Speaking to Luna was the equivalent of speaking to a ninety-year-old Alzheimer's patient. Every sentence led into a convoluted mess of logic that only she and her sisters seemed to comprehend.

"I promise, I'm not questioning you, or any of your sisters. I just want to understand." Nevin was half telling the truth. He was totally questioning these women's life choices, but he was sincere in his desire to understand.

Mike mumbled something unintelligible as more and more blood seeped from the opened wounds on his face and neck. He slightly shifted, causing his lip to fall in the dirt at his side.

"Suffering is God in this place, Nevin. I assumed you already knew that, considering what we've shown you." Luna gestured towards Mike. "My sisters and I were born from suffering; we've known nothing but. Our mothers knew pain and suffering at the hands of our two fathers, as did we."

Luna and the rest of her sisters looked towards the ground, almost shamefully. "Some would label my sisters and I a 'pain worshiping cult', but that isn't true; not entirely. We aren't a cult. We are a family, a *real* family." The group of sisters dropped their weapons, locking hands and bowing their heads. Nevin stuck his hands back into his pants pockets, feeling awkward and left out.

"That's why we took him. You know that, right?" Celeste blurted out loudly over the sound of the other sisters humming. Celeste reacted to the look given to her by her older sister like someone had just hit her in the chest with a sledgehammer. Nevin wondered what Celeste had meant by her comment.

"Took who?" Nevin asked, looking around like whoever they were talking about was on their way to join in on the conversation.

Luna dropped her sister's hand, not saying a word as she picked up the baseball bat wrapped in barbed wire that Pluto had been holding moments ago.

"Kill him now. No more questions, no more talking." She shoved the baseball bat into Nevin's chest, the barbs digging deeply into his sternum.

"Shit!" Nevin grunted, pulling the bat free from his shirt. He looked down at Mike, who looked dead already. He wasn't a bad guy. In his mind he was simply living, getting the most experiences he could out of life. How many people can say they've done anything remotely close to the things he's done in the past few hours? Not very fucking many, that's for sure.

Luna reached towards Nevin, running her fingers across the little bloody tears in his shirt. He thought back to when Luna flashed him her thick, smelly bush. This chick was fucking batshit, and Nevin knew that she was going to want his cock inside of her unwashed pussy. He wondered if he would be able to get hard for a chick, especially one with such a rough looking exterior. But what if he couldn't get hard? What if he couldn't pump babies into these crazy bitches? They would cut his cock off and toss it in the nearest pile of human waste.

"Kill him now, or you'll die at his side." Luna wasn't playing around. She wanted to see Nevin finish off his fourth best friend in the world.

He sighed, gripping the bat tightly. *Just close your eyes and pretend you're beating the shit out of a watermelon,* he thought to himself, taking a few steps closer to Mike.

There was a foul smell of fresh shit radiating from Mike's direction. It made his stomach do backflips. He noticed all the sisters locking hands again. They smiled at him, excited for the candy that would spew from this macabre pinata.

"You- you always were a naive, self-centered, pretty-" Mike's final insults fell short when the barbed wire bat connected with the side of his head. Nevin opened his eyes to see one of Mike's ears hanging from the deadly wire. He closed his eyes, taking another swing, hoping it would be his last.

CRACK!

Mike's head jerked so violently to the right that his neck snapped, and the gash that the saw blade had given him opened wider, causing his head to dangle like a broken Pez dispenser. The girls cheered in jubilation, jumping up and down, rushing over to collect handfuls of the blood that squirted up from the spot that Mike's head once sat. Strangely, Nevin thought back to the blowjob that Mike had given him in the car.

"I want you to come and see the children," Luna whispered in Nevin's ear, taking his hand in hers, pulling him back towards the house as her sisters celebrated.

Man, when I'm old and grey, this will be one hell of a story to tell the grandkids. Most people feel that they've accomplished something just by visiting the Grand Canyon. But this, this is living life to the fullest. Nevin's inner monologue lasted until he and Luna reached the top of the stairs inside the old farmhouse.

Luna turned to face Nevin as they stood in front of the closed door that led to the baby room. "They're sweet girls, and they'll all grow to appreciate suffering the same as my sisters and I."

A million scenarios played in his mind, but nothing could prepare him for what he would see once Luna opened *that* door. The room was dark and warm, the odor of baby shit and piss smacked Nevin in the face so hard that he had to pull his T-shirt up to help block the smell. Luna walked across the dark room until she reached the window where a giant black tarp blocked out the sunlight. She gave a quick tug, then the tarp fell to the floor.

"Fuck me." Nevin whispered to himself as his brain began to take in every inch of the atrocities surrounding him. The floor was covered in dirty, naked babies. Some looked the age of toddlers, all sleeping in filthy piles of shit and garbage. This wasn't what Nevin wanted to see. This wasn't something he wanted to remember.

"I- I- I don't understand." Nevin had just sacrificed his gay lover in the most sadistic fashion. He had seen the fucked-up shit on sites like Rotton.com back in the day. Hell, he had even done some pretty fucked up shit that his friends and family would disown him for. Like the time he had intentionally poisoned the new puppy his grandpa had adopted for him when he was eight. But this, this was beyond anything he had ever seen or experienced.

"There are- there are so many of them." Nevin started to feel dizzy. He used the shit covered wall to hold himself up. Just when he thought he had seen the worst of this house of fucking horrors, he saw something else that made him have to turn and vomit all over the already disgusting floor.

"Chains! Fucking- wha- *fuckingchains?*"

Luna smiled, taking a few steps towards Nevin after having to step over a few sleeping infants. "My sisters and I fed on filth and squalor when we were this age, and it made us the strong women that we are today. These beautiful young women will grow to know pain better than any man who comes poking his filthy noes where it doesn't belong."

She seemed to be growing increasingly defensive at Nevin's lack of understanding. Nevin looked back down at the chains around each child's neck, the chains that acted as leashes, the chains attached to thick metal rings bolted into floor.

"This isn't my Grand Canyon." Nevin blurted out as he dry-heaved even harder. Luna tilted her head like a confused Saint Bernard. "Alright, lets get the fucking out of the way so that I can hit the road. I've seen enough to last a fucking lifetime."

Luna only grew more and more confused as Nevin continued on. "I told you that I would be part of this, and hey, I'm all about it. So, I'll fuck who I have to fuck, then I have to hit the road."

Luna began laughing, realizing that Nevin was under the illusion that this was some fun, fucked up trip he could tell his friends on the internet about.

"Do you think this is some kind of fucking brothel? You can just show up, let out your inner psycho, bust a nut, and fucking leave!?"

Nevin shrugged his shoulders, wiping the vomit from his chin. "Have you ever seen that show, 'Westworld?'" Luna tilted her head again, clenching her fists as well. "I guess not. But I thought it was kind of like that. I mean, I brought a disposable friend, I killed him like you wanted me to, and I totally get why I had to do that." Nevin raised his hands defensively, smiling to ease the tension. "You had me kill him so that I couldn't go and snitch on you and your crazy little cult, I totally get it. And look, I'll still fuck whoever you want me to fuck, that was part of the deal and I'm a man of my word, Baby girl."

Luna had killed many men in her life, more than any single woman in history no doubt. Most of them came to the farm thinking they had stumbled upon a bunch of helpless girls who needed a big strong man to take care of them, some a little crazed and sex hungry, but she had never encountered a man as strange as Nevin.

"Are you alright in the head?" Luna asked, stepping over another baby.

Nevin looked around with a smile. "Am *I* alright in the head? *You* of all people are asking *me* if *I'm* crazy?"

That question always bugged Nevin. He had been poked and prodded by those fucking doctors his entire life, his fucking mom and dad always telling him that he needed serious help. They went behind his back and told every guy that he ever brought home to watch themselves, that he wasn't normal. "Those motherfuckers!" Nevin shouted out, not realizing where he was at that moment. The sound of babies crying yanked him back to reality.

"You fucking woke them!" Luna growled, using her foot to push one of the babies back into the heap. Nevin heard the floorboards creak behind him, he turned to catch the butt of a rifle to the forehead, knocking him out.

"He's fucking weird, but violent. He'll make good children for Celeste and Jupiter. Take him down to the basement, I'm sure he and Paul will get along just fine."

Chapter Six

Neglect is a Bitch, and So Are You

The cabin started to fucking stink like death, and it was originating from underneath Mary-Ann's bedroom door. Mary-Ann and Franny had gone down to the creek to fill some buckets of water, that little house on the prairie type bullshit that we had all grown accustomed to. I awoke on the hardwood floor, completely naked. This was nothing new, it was just how I had always slept. Something about sleeping on a hard, uncomfortable surface made me feel a sense of satisfaction when I woke the next day, my dick would instantly grow hard the second I rolled over on my back. Mary-Ann had always frowned upon me for sleeping in such a way, but after seeing my cock and bare ass every day for fifteen or sixteen years, it becomes the norm. Every foster parent would cuss me out and spank my ass with a belt every single time they caught me nude and asleep on their bathroom floor. The spankings became sort of a morning bonus that came with a stiff little cock that I could play with under the breakfast table. But, back to this fucking smell.

"What in the fuck?" I sat up, scratching the taint that I hadn't washed in the past two weeks. I was familiar with the smell of a rotting corpse. Did I find the smell to be pleasant? Fuck no. Anyone who tells you otherwise is a fucking stuck-up, edgy fuck boy who writes about babies being raped and murdered, thinking he's 'too extreme for the average reader'.

I looked around, wondering if we had finally resorted to cannibalism. Jasper died in the shed, I checked on him a few days after Franny and I sodomized and raped him, his corpse all curled up in the corner of the old shed, his pretty boy face now resembling the crypt keepers. I thought about leaving him, but decided I might want to turn the shed into a fuck shack for future hikers that decide to stop by.

I dragged the body, with both of the severed legs tucked into Jasper's faggy little hiker's bag over towards a small sinkhole that sat about ten feet from the back of the cabin. I managed to stuff Jasper down into the hole and cover him with some old pieces of plywood. As I stood in the kitchen, ass naked, looking out through the back window, I noticed the plywood had been moved. Did Franny cook pieces of that motherfucker and feed them to me? If so, it hadn't yet made me shit all over the kitchen floor.

"Mary-Ann." I said out loud, turning to look towards her bedroom door at the end of the hall. As I walked down the hall, my dick no-longer solid, I wondered what I would find in Mary-Ann's bedroom. As soon as I pushed open the door, a repugnant, foul smell shot straight up my nostrils and dry-humped my brain like a full syringe of potassium chloride.

Why would someone like Mary-Ann bring a corpse into her own bedroom? She didn't partake in the extracurricular activities that I took part in from time-to-time. Well, not that I was aware of.

I looked under the bed and in the closet, but only found a few pairs of underwear that I would lick the crotch of before tossing them to the side. The smell of Mary-Ann's day-old pussy couldn't block out the stench of rotted flesh that had begun to make my eyes water.

Suddenly, from the corner of my right eye, I saw it. I leaned forward, my ass crack spreading wide open. There was a fucking human head stuffed underneath Mary-Ann's dresser. It was wrapped tightly in a pink towel that was now soaked in smelly, brown, liquid flesh. The wood floor where the head had been sitting was now stained black, little maggots squirmed as the sunlight hit them. The head wasn't the only thing wrapped up nicely in a pretty pink towel.

"What in the fuck is that?" I asked myself out loud, holding up the thick brown chunk that looked like a petrified turd. "That's a cock." I whispered, examining the mummified male member. I put my nose to it, instantly smelling Mary-Ann's special scent. I wondered if I had time to lean over the bed and fuck myself up the ass with Mary-Ann's toy, but the front door of the cabin opened. Here I was standing in Mary-Ann's bedroom, completely naked, rock solid, and holding a severed penis. I'll admit, I've been caught doing much worse.

"What are you doing in here?" Mary-Ann's voice trailed across the room. I looked up at her, still holding her cock toy up to the light coming from the window.

"I never in a million years thought I would have to ask you this question, but here it goes. Why, Mary-Ann? Why do you have severed body parts tucked under your dresser? And why is it a head and cock?"

I sat my bare ass on Mary-Ann's bed, still holding the pink towel containing the head under my left arm. Mary-Ann clenched her fists, I could hear her teeth grinding under her tightly pursed lips.

"Why can't I have anything in this world without *you* sticking your fucking nose in it? Who the fuck are *you* to judge *me*?"

Franny came walking up behind Mary-Ann, placing her hand on her shoulder. "What's wrong?" she asked, noticing the towel under my arm and the severed cock in my hand.

"Mary-Ann, can you at least explain to Franny, why it is that you have such items hidden away in your room, smelling up the place that we have to live in?" I braced myself for whatever Mary-Ann was going to throw at me, but she stood still enough to catch flies on her tongue. "Do you realize how fucking disgusting it is to shove shit like this up your cunt?"

Maybe the pot shouldn't be questioning the kettle about its color, but I had the right to know what was going through my little sister's head. "Maybe I haven't been the best influence on a young mind." I tucked the cock back in the towel with the head.

"Influence?" Mary-Ann whispered, her eyes turning rabid. "You think that you hold any type of influence over me, Paul? I want to be *nothing* like you, fucking *nothing*. You killed our foster family, you dragged me out in the middle of nowhere with this crazy fucking cunt." Mary-Ann smacked Franny's hand from her shoulder, then took a step further into the bedroom. "You have ruined my life, Paul. I should be going to prom and dating boys, making my own fucking mistakes in life. But no, I'm stuck here with you, wasting away what should be the best years of my fucking life. If you weren't aware of this, I will happily let you know, I fucking hate you, Paul. So many nights I've laid awake thinking about ways of killing you in your sleep. I've daydreamed about stomping on your fucking head while you're asleep on the floor like a fucking mental patient off their fucking meds! Do you hear me, Paul? Do you hear what I'm fucking saying to you!? I fucking despise you on a cellular level! I would saw through my own leg with a rusty hack saw if it would mean you dropping dead tight fucking now! I have no mother because of you, I have no father because of you, I have no one, all because of *you*! And as for the fucking head and cock, it was all I could get from the body you stuffed in a sinkhole, a body already completely devoured by wolves. I was going to take those body parts and hand them to the first cop I found when I finally escaped from you and this fucking island prison that you've kept me locked away in."

To my surprise, Franny was the first one to speak up after Mary-Ann's poor excuse of a performance. "You would rat out your own brother? What kind of evil person would do that to their own family?"

Mary-Ann would have fallen to the floor in laughter if she hadn't used the bedroom door as a crutch. "You're fucking joking, right? You fucking have to be joking." Mary-Ann lost her balance, falling to the floor and quite literally rolled in laughter. "Shit like that coming from someone like *you*!" Mary-Ann howled, pointing up at Franny as she held her stomach and kicked her feet like she was on an invisible bicycle.

"What is so funny? Why is she laughing like that, Paul? Do you think she's finally lost her mind?" Franny asked as I tossed Jasper's head and cock into the tree line.

I turned, handing Franny the pink towel. "She's a teenager who says retarded shit. It's a cry for attention." I shrugged, using Franny's shirt to wipe my hands. "I said some pretty outlandish shit when I was her age, probably runs in the family. Hold on to that towel, I'm going to wash up in the creek. I'll need it when I'm finished.

"Want some company?" Franny asked, rubbing her free hand through the slit between her tits.

"No. Now fuck off and keep an eye on Mary-Ann at the cabin." I turned and walked towards the small running creek.

I bathed myself in the creek, listening to the sounds of the birds above me as I floated peacefully on my back. Little did I know Mary-Ann would finally get the balls to run after ten long years. The next day, after a minor disagreement, she ran straight for the pig farm that we had been staring at for over a fucking decade. How in the fuck was I supposed to know that my life was about really fucking suck for the next few weeks?

I found myself chained up in the basement while Mary-Ann's sweet, virgin pussy was beaten and bloodied by two retarded hillbillies that I would soon kill. Not to mention I would later shoot Franny in the head and feed her to a bunch of hogs after she put a bullet in Mary-Ann's stomach.

Well, you know the fucking story.

It wasn't until years later when I returned to that very pig farm, expecting to find a familiar place where I could relax and collect my thoughts, but holy fuck, I was dead wrong. I guess I should have stopped being the overly predictable prick that I always had been. Because now, I'm chained up in a deeper part of that very same fucking basement. It was hidden behind an old cellar door underneath the stairs that I hadn't noticed during my first visit. All I remember before being chained up in the dark and forced to fuck crazy bitch after crazy bitch, was being dragged past a small room containing a desktop computer sitting on an old metal desk. I guess these bitches used it to lure fresh dick out to the middle of nowhere.

Chapter Seven

TITS OF THE MOTHER

"WHO ARE WE SENDING first?" Venus asked her older sister as they dragged Nevin's unconscious body down the basement steps of the old farmhouse. Luna stopped for a moment to take a break; she wiped a bead of sweat from her forehead before it could drip down into her eye. She was twenty-eight, and not getting any younger.

"I haven't decided yet. Who is the readiest?" Luna bent down to pick up Nevin's legs as they continued down the steps and into the darkness.

"Celeste and Jupiter are the youngest, and both have only had three children a piece. I just had twins, if you remember. It certainly shouldn't be me." Venus added, starting to feel Nevin's deadweight as they reach the cement floor.

"Regardless of who is next, it won't be Paul giving them a baby this time around. Have you noticed that they're all born so small? For such a large man, he make's the tiniest babies."

Luna pulled an old piece of plywood out of the way, revealing the door that led to the cellar. The basement was used mostly as a 'timeout' area for the younger children who acted out. Venus smiled at the two young girls currently being deprived of their privileges.

"I hope you two are learning how to get along and play by the rules." She nodded to them as they lifted their heads off the cold, unforgiving floor. They stared at the mother figures like caged animals, even going as far as to growl. "Maybe more time will do you some good."

Venus turned back to Luna as the cellar door was pulled open. "Do you think the two of them might be retarded? I can't remember who birthed them." She put her finger on her lip, trying to remember.

"Never mind that. I need your help." Luna huffed frustratingly at her younger sibling. "I would have asked Neptune to help if I had known you were going to use your brain instead of brawn."

The cellar was much darker than the basement above, only a few lightbulbs hung from the ceiling in the front room.

The smell that lingered would have been too much for the average person to handle, but the sisters had grown quite used to it.

"We'll need more gas for the generator." Luna placed her hands on her hips, staring into the tiny room that housed the computer. "Sheriff Rhea was generous enough to provide us with the means to reach the outside world. Don't abuse the gifts given to us."

Luna felt that she had to constantly play mother to her younger siblings, she even recalled breast feeding them years ago.

"I'm sure the Sheriff will be by in the next few days to check on things. I don't want her to leave here as unhappy as she did the last time, when we had to explain what happened to that farmer who brought the pigs." Even in the hot, dry cellar, a chill ran down Venus's spine.

"I understand, Luna. I'll talk to the others and make sure they understand the importance of saving our resources." She lowered her head, knowing she would surely be spanked for Luna having to remind her of something a second time. It was strange to Venus, the thought of worshiping pain and suffering but to also being threatened with it.

Luna unlocked the sliding metal door in front of her, dragging it along its tracks until it hit the stopper with a loud clank. The room was dark, a single light bulb only illuminating a few feet of the dirt covered cement floor. The sound of chains being dragged could be heard from the far-left corner. A man appeared from the shadows, shackles secured tightly around his ankles and wrists, with thick, silverplated padlocks. The man was very tall, maybe six-five or six-six, dark smudges of dirt smeared in spots on his large muscular arms. He had grown a thick beard and long hair in the time he had been here. Luna couldn't recall how long it had been. The large man was barefoot, wearing faded blue jeans and a black T-shirt with the sleeves torn off. He took another step forward, having to duck under a pipe on the ceiling. Luna's heart raced.

"Hello, Paul," she said with smile, clearing her dry throat.

"It's been a long time since I last seen you, Bitch. For the past few years, I've seen nothing but your equally ugly sisters coming down here to feed me and empty my shit bucket. When's the last time I fucked one of those babies in you? Did you miss me? I *bet* you fucking did."

Luna cleared her throat again, wishing she had brought the tranquilizer gun that the sheriff had given her. Paul had been shot many times with that very gun, like a rabid dog tied up in the backyard.

"You going to shoot me with that dart gun again?" Paul looked at Venus, then back at Luna. He smiled a devious smile.

"What did you do to yourself, there on your forehead?" Luna asked, trying to get a better look at the fresh scar.

Paul used his pointer finger to rub the spot that Luna was referring to. "Oh, this? Yeah, I was feeling like daddy around here, figured I might as well look like the kind of daddy you girls get wet over."

Luna noticed that the little scar on Paul's head matched the same scar that Charles Manson and his followers burned into *their own* foreheads with the flame heated ends of a screwdriver.

"Wait a second, I got it all wrong, didn't I? Your daddy never looked like this. I remember your daddy's being two dumb, butt ass ugly, inbred pig fuckers that I killed in this very house. I had spent years in that cabin listening to you little whores being fucked and tortured day in and day out. Shit was sweet music to my ears. Tell me, did one of your dads ever make you fuck that big ass pig they let run around the house? I think his name was, Salsa, right?"

Luna rubbed her sweaty hands together, looking over at Venus to roll her eyes. She and her sisters had these very same insults thrown at them every time they opened the cellar door.

"Keep rolling those eyes, Bitch. Keep pissing me off, and you and I are going to have a fuck party with a bottle of whisky and a chainsaw. A chill ran down Luna's spine.

"We've brought you some company. Someone not nearly as psychotic as you, but he's crazy, violent, and best of all, fertile."

Venus butted in, walking slowly over to join at the side of her older sister. Paul glanced over at the unconscious man lying by the door.

"Something about this farm makes all you bitches act like you've got it all figured out, shit never changes." Paul chuckled, yanking playfully on his shackles.

"Is that what happened to Franny and Mary-Ann? They acted as if they had it all figured out? Is that why you fed them both to the hogs?"

Paul took a few steps forward, but his chains kept him from going much further. "You have a god complex, don't you, bitch? You think you can cast me down to this hell to be your fucking servant? I've had about enough of it. If I had known you nasty cunts had made yourselves at home here, I would have come better prepared. Who would've thought I'd catch a brick to the side of the fucking head only to wake up chained to the fucking floor? Funny how things work out, huh?"

Venus and Luna shared a smile at Paul's expense. "We've told you before, Paul. We are not your enemy. We love and apricate the wonderful things you've done, all the pain and suffering you've caused." Luna started rubbing her breasts, Venus stood by and watched her sister, licking her lips at the beautiful sight she felt privileged to behold. "You've killed so many people, caused so much pain." Luna moved her hand down to her crotch, rubbing her fingers on it until her eyes rolled back.

"Jesus fucking Christ, you're one weird bitch." Paul muttered stepping back into his dark corner of the room while watching Luna finish herself off.

"You want pain, Bitch? I'll show you pain." Paul whispered to himself, imagining the amount of destruction he would cause if he could get the fuck out of his shackles.

"I'm going to cum!" Luna cried out, her body tensing up as she moaned at the top of her lungs.

"I love you, big sister!" Venus cried out, rejoicing in this celebratory moment. What Venus didn't realize was Nevin waking up, rubbing his head in confusion. Paul was the first to notice, hoping like hell that-

"What now, Bitch!?" Nevin screamed, tackling Venus from behind, knocking her to the ground in the center of the floor. Luna looked up from her back at the swinging lightbulb above, then suddenly, a shadow was cast over her.

"Hey, how's it going?" Paul asked, that devious smile returning.

"Help!" Was all Venus could say before she was yanked up by her neck, the steel chains wrapped tightly around her throat. Luna turned to run towards the door, wondering where she had left the tranquilizer gun, but something grabbed ahold of her arm, jerking her forcibly back into the room, dislocating her shoulder.

"Looks like I'm going to have one hell of a story to tell the grandkids after all." Nevin smiled, grabbing Luna by her hair, smashing her face into one of the steel support beams. "You still want that fucking?" Nevin asked, licking the side of Luna's bloody face. He used both hands to crack Luna's face into the steel beam once more, knocking out a few of her front teeth. "I can tell the neighbors all about the crazy vacation I took!" Nevin laughed hysterically as Luna spit broken shards of teeth on the floor.

"Hey!" Nevin turned to see Paul Homolka, Venus on her knees in front of him, her face turning a dark purple. "There is a room with a computer, down that hall." Paul nodded towards the door. "Go and find the keys." Paul ordered, making sure to give Nevin a smile that told him that he could be trusted.

"I'm such a huge fan of yours! I've seen every documentary, every cold-case episode, I even have a few shell casings from the 1911 you used! I got them on E-bay for like, two-hundred-bucks or something!"

Paul could feel the back of his neck growing hot from frustration, but this dumb fuck was his only chance of escaping this fucking cellar. He *had* to play it cool.

"That's great, Homo, now go find the fucking keys!"

Nevin nodded, scrambling to his feet as Luna lay beaten and unconscious on the cellar floor. "None of my friends are going to believe this!" he cheered, sprinting down the hallway until he found the room with the computer.

"I'm going to kill you, then I'm going to have some fun with your cunt, matriarch of a sister over there on the floor." Paul whispered, yanking Venus to her feet using his shackles. "I'm going to eradicate you, and every other bitch on this property, Afterwards, I'm going to watch this place burn."

Venus used her hands to try to relieve some of the pressure around her throat. "The- baby- babies-"

Paul tightened his grip, causing the veins in Venus' forehead to pulsate. "The babies? Oh, yeah, the babies. I guess they're going to learn the meaning of death a litter earlier than expected." Paul laughed, lifting Venus off her feet. She kicked and squirmed, gasping for even the smallest breath. "Consider yourself lucky. Your sisters won't have it so fucking easy."

Venus stopped kicking, her arms falling limp at her side, a stream of dark yellow piss ran down her leg and onto the floor. Paul turned her body, laughing at the strangulated expression on her lifeless face. Paul tossed the corpse aside, growing impatient at Nevin's lack of hustle.

"I found the keys!" Nevin called out, sprinting back into the room with a small set of keys that he dangled above his head.

"Great, now give them to me so that I can kill the rest of the nasty cunts living in this baby factory." Paul reached for the keys, but Nevin stopped just out of arms reach.

"You're not going to kill me, are you? Cause that shit wouldn't be very cool considering I'm the one who helped you get free. Do I have your word that I get to watch you kill all these bitches, and go free *after*?"

Paul rolled his eyes. "Yes, I promise that I won't kill you, and also yes to you being allowed to watch me commit mass genocide on an entire community. Now, give me those fucking keys."

Nevin smiled, tossing the keys to Paul.

"All these fucking years I've had to sit down here and listen to those cunts running back and forth up there. I've been eating their shitty fucking stew every goddamn day of the week, shitting like a pregnant Mexican bitch over a fucking bucket."

The locks on Paul's wrists and ankles sat in a pile on top of the chains that he had been wearing, he stepped forward with a smile. "You haven't seen a chainsaw lying around, have you?" Paul asked, starting to feel like his old self again.

"The girls, they have all sorts of crazy fucking weapons in the living room. Some of them are really fucked up, homemade ones. I think a chainsaw may be a little tame for these chicks." Nevin added, rubbing the huge lump on his head. Paul had almost forgotten about-

"Sheriff? Please, please, you have to come quick." Paul and Nevin both looked down at the spot where Luna had been lying motionless.

"Sneaky cunt." Paul whispered, crossing his arms and leaning against the wall behind Luna. She had dragged herself down to the small room with the computer, she had the receiver of C.B radio in her hand.

"You're going to be right back in the dark, chained up for another-"

Paul kicked Luna hard on the side of the head, pancaking it between his foot and the metal desk.

"I truly have no fucking interest in how goddamn long I've been locked up down here. But I'll let you in on a little something that *does* pique my interest." Paul knelt down next to Luna; her eyes glazed over. "I'm interested to see how loud you can scream."

Chapter Eight

The Pig Farm Massacre

(Content Warning)

I've killed a fucking ton of people in my time, some I don't even remember doing so. It always sucks to get a boring kill. You know when you jerk off, and that nut doesn't feel as great as it usually does? It feels like wasted time, and a wasted load. Well, this kill, wasn't a wasted load, not even close. Luna screamed like a skinned housecat.

"I thought you worshiped this shit, Bitch?"

I peeled the meat from her back, exposing the muscle underneath. The fucking dipshit that had helped free me vomited all over the computer desk at sight of my draping Luna's flesh over my shoulders like a warm, cunt-coat. I slapped Luna's exposed fascia, she screamed loud enough to wake the dead.

"All that connective tissue found below the skin, stabilizing, imparting strength, maintaining vessel patency, it's all just buttons to cause unimaginable pain and torment."

Luna tried to turn her head to look back at me, her lips were cracked and bleeding, her face even more pale than it had been before. "Kill me, you fucking son of a bitch." she begged, the blood vessels in her eyes had all but exploded.

I grabbed her greasy fucking hair, yanking her head back, putting my lips to her neck. "I'm going to fucking devour you, you hear me? I'm going to hurt you so fucking bad. When I'm done, I'm going to kill every fucking one of those nasty cunts upstairs. I want you to know that before you decide to die like the weak, pathetic, false prophet you are. I don't want to kill you fast, Baby." I licked the foul-tasting sweat from her cheek before reaching my hand over and grabbing one of her perky little titties. "You don't even get me hard."

I laughed, reaching for the rusty box cutter that I had found in the desk drawer, the same one I had just used to skin Luna's back. "Would you mind if I wore you when killing your sisters and all that bastard offspring?"

Luna tried to scream again, but I slid the blade from her bellybutton, down to her hairy cunt, I then slid my hands inside the incision. "Kill me! I'm begging you."

I shook my head, finally feeling my dick start to poke against the inside of my blue jeans. I massaged inside the gash, playing a little wax on, wax off. I grabbed a corner of the gash, pulling it with all my strength, ripping a giant sheet of flesh from Luna's cunt. I glanced down at the human leather in my hand, Lunas's hairy pussy lips sat atop of it. "That's fucking foul."

I showed the dipshit what I had collected, his face turned a shade of green before vomiting again. "Use it to wipe your face off, you look disgusting." I tossed the flap of flesh onto the computer desk, smiling at my new *friend*.

"Wipe my face with it?" the dipshit asked, looking at me like a confused child.

I slammed my fist down on the metal desk. "Did I *fucking* stutter? Wipe your fucking face off, or I'll shove that mound of pussy down your throat."

The dipshit looked down at the flesh mound, picking it up in his right hand. I noticed little stray pussy hairs lying on the desk.

"It's all part of the experience, I guess." The rat faced cuck put the flesh up to his face. "It smells like rotten tuna."

I rolled my eyes at the little prick's complaint. "Before you wipe your disgusting face, what the fuck is your name? I keep calling you *the little prick*, in my mind."

The little prick looked up excitedly, hoping I would just forget the whole wiping his face with smelly pussy meat.

"It's um, Nevin. I came here with a friend after-"

"Great, I don't need your autobiography, *Homo*. Wipe you face before *I'm* the one throwing up."

Nevin nodded his pretty boy head, wiping the vomit from his mouth with the pussy. When he was finished, I couldn't help but laugh at the beard of wet pussy hair he left behind on his upper lip.

"That's a good boy, Nevin. Now, watch and learn."

Nevin nodded stupidly. I grabbed Luna around the throat lifting her up so that she was bent over the desk, her face lying in a puddle of Nevin's puke. I lifted the back of her stupid gown up, which was now completely drenched in blood and piss. I leaned over, putting my nose in the asshole that looked just as hairy as the pussy had. Nevin gazed in horror at the sight of me ramming my tongue deep into Luna's ass, grabbing her hips to stabilize her shaky frame. It tasted like a mouth full of dirty pennies that you scraped out of the cup holder of an old Station Wagon.

"It must suck, eh? Experiencing something that should feel wonderful but being in too much pain to enjoy it. That has to suck." I laughed, sliding my tongue up Luna's crack before using the box cutter to slice through her Achilles tendons.

"ARGH!" Luna dropped to her knee's, crying out, begging me to kill her.

"All those years you kept me locked away in the dark, shooting me with that fucking dart gun, making me fuck your nasty fucking sisters! This shit is Sesame Street right now, Cunt Bitch!" I stomped as hard as I could on Luna's ankle, shattering it with ease. "You want to know what pain is!?" I screamed in the queen bitch's face as she cried.

"Was that Silence of the Lambs?"

I looked up at Nevin, my eyebrow raised curiously. "What?" I asked.

"What you just said, that was quote from the movie, Silence of the Lambs. Have you not seen that one?" Nevin placed his hands firmly on his hips.

"To be honest, Nevin, I've been a little pre-occupied over the last 30 something years. Not much time to sit and watch your retarded fucking movies."

Nevin sighed dramatically. "Well, you should check it out, I think it's right up your alley."

Was this fucking guy for real? I couldn't tell if he was fucking with me, or if he was genuinely autistic.

"Yeah, Nevin, I'll check it out sometime." I rolled my eyes, wondering if this was what the world had become in my time of being locked away as a fuck slave. Were all the people in the outside world like this fucking guy? Did they all dress the way that he did? Was there some kind of chemical spill that I was unaware of?

To keep my mind occupied, I used the boxcutter to remove all the skin from the lower neck and up, making a full-head, Luna mask. The bitch was still breathing before I had Nevin lift the desk so that I could place Luna's head under it.

"Drop it." I commanded Nevin as he strained to hold up the heavy metal desk. Luna's skull made a loud crunching sound, like a bag of peanuts being crushed under a car tire. The computer rocked violently, crashing and exploding on the floor below. I pulled Luna's face over my own, having to slit the back of the hairline a bit to make it fit comfortably.

"That is the most horrifying thing that I've ever seen in my life." Nevin added, his eyes wide with surprise.

I approached him slowly, just to give an added effect. "When we go up there, I will ask you to do things for me, and you will do them without hesitation, understand? Until I get a decent weapon, you are my extra set of hands, got that?"

Nevin nodded, coming off weirdly excited.

We climbed the steps that led up to the basement, the change in temperature felt fucking amazing. "It's been a while." I looked around, noticing the two, very young girls chained up in the exact spot that *I* had been, all those years ago.

"This is where those farmers kept you, the same place you killed them, and Mary-Ann."

A sharp pain coursed through my head like a bolt of electricity. "Fuck." I muttered, placing my hand on my forehead, having to remove Luna's face.

"It's probably the pressure difference." Nevin added, shrugging his muscular shoulders.

I glanced at him through my fingers. "What in the fuck are you even talking about? I wasn't two-hundred miles under the fucking ocean, genius. You're not seriously *that* fucking stupid, are you?"

Nevin shrugged his shoulders once more, a blank, clueless expression on his face.

"Jesus Christ." I shook my head, clearly embarrassing Nevin.

"He's the one that the mothers kept under the floor." One of the little blonde girls whispered to the other. Their whispering stopped as I drew closer. They both wore those white fucking gowns that the others wore, only *theirs* looked as if they had been locked up down here for *some time* now. I made it close enough to reach down and stroke their little, flushed cheeks. They didn't look afraid of me, just curious.

"Do you girls know who I am to you?" I asked, playing with my food before taking a big bite.

They looked at each other for a moment, then back at me. One of them I now noticed didn't actually have blonde hair, more like a very light brown. "I bet you two are the first from me. I can see the resemblance." I smiled, running my fingers through my beard.

"Where are our mothers? We saw them bring that one down to the cellar where you lived." The brown-haired girl pointed towards Nevin. "By the way, I'm Thebe, and this is my sister, Europa." The blonde sister noted, placing her hand on her sister's shoulder.

"Well, Thebe, I killed those two bitches down in the cellar."

Thebe and Europa stared up at me, their emotions, impossible to read. "Did they suffer?" Europa asked, reaching forward, placing her hand on *my* shoulder.

I took her hand in mine, seeing myself in the darkness of her eyes. For a moment I felt lost, like I had been falling for hours, only now to be stuck, floating in the nothingness of the abyss. "Yeah, they suffered, they suffered really bad." I admitted, not expecting the reaction I received.

"Good. They would have preferred it that way. If they died suffering, they died happy. Isn't that right, Thebe?" Thebe nodded with a smile.

"What in the fuck is up with these fucking people?" I asked myself out loud. The girls giggled, almost as if they had never heard someone cuss before.

"Why are the two of you chained up like this?" I asked, lifting Europa's wrist to examine the shackle.

"Thebe and I broke the rules, now we're being punished. The two of us tend to hiss and growl any time someone gets onto us about acting up."

I laughed but wasn't exactly sure as to *why*. "I break the rules myself sometimes. But I've never been punished for doing it."

My bad leg started acting up, so I pushed myself up using my knuckles. "Look, I'm going to burn this place down. You and your sister here will either die from the smoke, or the house caving in on top of you. Would that kind of death be suitable for you two? Doesn't seem like a very *'painful'* way to go out, does it?"

The sisters looked in each other's eyes, like they were speaking to one another without saying a word. "That wouldn't be ideal." Europa finally responded, sadness in her voice.

Nevin cleared his throat in the background. "They don't *have* to die though, do they? Can't we just let them out?" I charged Nevin, cracking him in the jaw with my elbow, sending him into an old shelf of cans against the basement wall.

"You're all fucking maggots? What makes *them* special? You are my fucking extra set of hands, so unless you learn sign-language in the next five minutes, I suggest you shut the fuck up and drop the emotional bullshit you carry around."

Nevin looked up from the floor, his bottom lip was split down the center. I kneeled down, my bum leg throbbing in pain. "I am a hired exterminator. You hear me, Fuck Boy? The day I was born was the day I was hired. I am the destroyer, a global fucking holocaust, you got that?" Nevin nodded his head. "Just because they came from my dick bag, doesn't mean that they matter anymore, or any less than the rest of the vermin upstairs."

Nevin nodded once more before I returned to the girls.

Pulling the boxcutter from my pocket. Unlike Luna, the little girls didn't scream as I cut them open, they continued looking in each other's eyes, even as I reached inside them to pull out their intestines. Nevin finally looked up from the little ball he had curled himself into, he fought with everything in him to not look over at the spot that the little girls had been sitting in.

"Are we going upstairs now?" He asked, his hands shaking uncontrollably.

"Not unless you want to go over and get your nut off in one of them."

Nevin dry heaved loudly, spitting up traces of stomach acid.

"They've been down there for far too long." I heard a woman's voice say as she opened the basement door and began her descent down the steps. I rushed to the side, hiding until she reached the bottom.

"What in the-"

I grabbed the bitch in a chokehold, lifted her up off her feet, then snapped her neck. The body went limp, I tossed it to the side like the trash that *it* was.

"More of them are coming, they're going to kill us!" Nevin cried, curing back up into a little pussy ball of a man.

"Get your ass up those steps before you end up like *that* bitch."

I grabbed Luna's face, pulling it back over my head. Nevin did as he was told, I followed closely behind him, hoping whatever waited behind that door, would get to *him,* before me.

CHAPTER NINE

A HIRED EXTERMINATOR

MY HUMAN SHIELD OPENED the basement door. The sunlight hit my face for the first time in over a decade. It took a moment for the room to come into focus; my headache returned quickly after it did. "Fuck." I growled, starting to feel nauseous.

"What's wrong?" Nevin asked, turning to me.

"Don't fucking worry about it! Keep your goddamn eyes ahead."

I used the wall to catch my balance. Being suffocated by darkness and mildew for that many years, must have been fucking with my senses. Nevin and I stood in the living room, voices could be heard above our heads.

"Goddamn, there's a fucking arsenal in here," I whispered to myself, still using Nevin as a shield. The living room was full of assault rifles, shotguns, knives of every variety, and many homemade weapons. "You said there was a bunch of homemade weapons. You didn't say these bitches had prepared for the next civil war."

Nevin looked around the room. "All of this extra stuff wasn't here before. They must've *just* put it here."

I picked up a large hunting knife that rested in a black leather sheath. I tucked it in my waistline, along with a police force issued beretta M9, and two extra clips. An M16 rested on the old, faded red sofa.

"Who said bitches don't provide?" I chuckled, checking to make sure the magazine was fully loaded in the M16.

"What do you think they're planning with all this?" Nevin asked, picking up a wooden baseball bat covered in shards of broken glass.

"It doesn't matter what they were planning. What matters is what *I'm* going to do next." I smiled, looking over towards the steps that led upstairs. "You know something? I almost bet that you don't make it out of here alive."

Nevin turned to me, his eyes bugging out of his thick skull. "I have to. I can't die here, Paul. If I don't make it out, who is going to tell these awesome fucking stories?"

I shook my head, still amazed that this fucker had made it as far as he had in his miserable life.

"If I die, Mike died for nothing." His head dropped. "He-he loved me, you know? He loved me and I didn't give a fuck about him."

I rolled my eyes, wishing I had slit his throat after killing Luna in the cellar. "Was Mike your fuck buddy or something? Did he suck on your cock every time you had one of these emotional outbursts? Maybe it was best that he died, dealing with you and your odd range of emotions is a fucking nightmare."

Nevin clenched his fist as his eyebrow furrowed. "Yeah, Paul, we were fucking faggots who sucked each other's dicks. I'm sure someone like you really loves killing twinks, don't you?"

I was really in the mood to do some killing, but Nevin was going to ruin the element of surprise with his pouting. "You told me that you were a fan, but it looks like you really don't know shit about me. I don't hate faggots. Hell, I've been known to fuck a man every now and again. I mean, it's not for pleasure, sex never is for me. I don't kill anyone because of who or what they fuck, I don't kill anyone based on race, skin-color, or beliefs. If you think about it, I'm the most non-discriminatory killer this world has ever seen. I kill everyone, and anyone. If you breath, I fucking hate you."

The steps creaked behind Nevin; a red-headed woman peeked curiously around the corner at us. Before she could blink, I raised the M16, putting a round in her forehead.

BANG!

The bitch's head jerked back as blood and brains hit the banister behind her. "It's show time." I shouted at the top of my lungs.

I darted towards the steps, jumping over the dead girls' body, reaching the top of the stairs in a matter of seconds.

"FUCKER!"

I turned to find another woman running towards me with an axe raised above her head.

BANG!

I aimed for her head, but the round caught her in the lower jaw. Half of her face exploded before she hit the ground.

"Get the fuck up here, Retard!" I shouted down the steps at Nevin, who I could hear crying like he had in the basement. "Goddamn it! I'm going to skin you alive, right after I kill the rest of these fucking cunts! You hear that, Ladies? Come out and see who's face I'm wearing!"

I kicked open a door, sending a shock wave through my bad leg. An empty bathroom sat before me, the smell of shit and piss must have been lingering behind the door for some time, waiting to escape out into the hall. I kicked another door, shooting the first thing that moved.

BANG! BANG!

I put two rounds in the chest of a woman standing in the corner holding a barbed wire bat. I noticed a blood chair in the middle of the room, dried blood on the floor beneath. I turned to the next door, ramming into it with my shoulder. "Fuck me!" I called out, three more women holding tightly to crying babies, each of them holding two at a time.

BANG!

I shot the closest woman in the head; she dropped the crying brats in a heap of trash on the floor. The other two women just stared at me, emotionless expressions on their faces. "What do you bitches think about my mask?" I asked before popping a round into the heavier set woman on the right.

BANG!

Two more babies dropped to the floor as the woman's body crumpled. "Aren't you going to smile? You finally get to be '*fucked*' by me again."

The woman tilted her head to the right, rocking the babies softly.

BANG! BANG! BANG!

Two rounds caught the woman in the neck, the other took the side of her head off. Now there was a room full of crying babies, causing that goddamn headache to come racing back. "What in the fuck is this headache!" I shouted, making the babies scream even louder.

I stepped on the hand of one of the babies under some old newspaper, her hair the same color black as mine. Even over the sound of nine or ten babies screaming their fucking lungs out, I could hear commotion coming from downstairs. I guess the rest of the woman had been out-side, now they were doing *fuck knows* to Nevin in the living room.

I peeked out the door, wondering if any of them were stupid enough to come up the stairs. I turned back to the screaming children, the fucking smell in the room was making me nauseous again. "You won't be screaming when I burn this fucking house down!" I shouted, kicking a hole in the wall that caused a swarm of rats to come piling out on top of each other. The vermin scurried around the room, looking for food, and a new place to hide. "Disgust-ing." I muttered before leaving the bedroom, closing the door behind me.

I had twenty-two rounds left in the M16, more than enough to take care of whoever was downstairs. Strangely, the commotion had stopped, I pictured them all waiting for me, guns at the ready. I had survived a firing squad in that asylum, I could *surely* survive this one.

"Come on down and leave them babies alone, you hear?" I stopped on the top step, regretting not stomping some heads in that bedroom before-

There was a loud pop, one I had heard many times over many years. "Damn it." I sighed, pulling the dart from

the back of my neck. I turned to see one of the women standing in the bathroom behind me, holding that fucking dart gun. I think I fell face first down the steps once the light disappeared.

"Paul!" I slowly opened my eyes to the sound of Nevin's faggy voice calling out to me. "Paul!" My neck was stiff, and a few ribs felt broken, but I seemed to be alive. I was no longer wearing Luna's face, which was a shame considering the pain in the ass it was to get it off Luna's head.

"Paul!" goddamn, what did that motherfucker want with me?

"What!?" I shouted, the world finally coming through my swollen eyes. I was handcuffed by one hand to a steel pipe attached to the side of the farmhouse. The remaining family members stood in a circle at the opening of the barn that I myself had never entered.

I smiled at the sight of Nevin, who was hog tied, and completely naked, his bare ass stuck straight up in the air. I thought these crazy whores needed him for his dick. What in the hell were they about to do to him?

"Paul! Please, please fucking help me!"

I rolled my eyes, which seemed to be a theme with this fucking guy. "What the fuck do you want me to do, Dumb Fuck? I'm handcuffed to a fucking pipe. But hey, I'm with you in spirit."

Nevin looked confused, like he had just noticed my current situation. "These fucking women are crazy!" he cried out, his face lying in the mud. I fought hard from rolling my eyes again, one of them was in a lot of pain.

"Yeah? No shit? When exactly did you come to that conclusion, Nevin? Please, I have to know!" I shouted, my condescending attitude going completely over his head. "I think they need you, so they're probably just going to torture you really bad, don't worry about it." Nevin began crying, my attempt at being humorous not helping his emotional state.

"You killed Luna." A voice came from beside me. I turned to see one of the women kneeling down beside me, her body odor causing my nose hairs to curl. I tried to wink, but my eye was fucked. "I'm not sure if you remember me, but I came to you when I was really young so that you could give me your seed."

I studied the smelly nutcase up and down with what little vison I had left. "You all look the same to me. I guess you looked a lot better when you were younger, eh?" I laughed, turning back to watch Nevin cry some more.

"You killed our daughter, you know that?" I turned back to the woman, wondering which of the many girls that I had slaughtered today, was her little bastard. "You pulled her insides out like she was some kind of wild animal."

I knew then who she had been referring to. "Oh, one of your bastards was in the basement. Let me ask, were they *both* mine? Cause let me tell you, they died without making a fucking peep. I found that pretty damn impressive, and the only person to ever impress *me*, was me."

I was hit hard in the knee with a baseball bat that had razor blades driven into it. The pain was comparable to stepping on a fucking landmine.

"You fucking cunt! Goddamn it!"

The hot, stale, summer air brushed against the wide opened gash in the center of my knee, the blood gushed out like the popped pimple of the chin of a fourteen-year-old boy. The woman moved closer, taking a handful of my beard in her hand before yanking downwards on it.

"My name is Pluto. You remember that, alright? I'm going to be the last fucking person that you ever know."

Through the pain, I gave Pluto a smile. "I can't fucking wait, Bitch." I flicked my tongue like a snake in her face. She smiled back, like she knew something that I didn't.

"I was one of the girls old enough to remember what you did on this farm all those years ago. My sister, Luna, and I, we watched you kill those two girls over by the pig pen. We even stayed watching after you hopped in our daddy's truck and drove off. You know, seeing those two girls in the pig pen is what pushed us to escape from the barn. We knew our daddies were dead. Who was going to hit us for leaving?" She pulled down harder on my beard.

"I've already heard this story from your dead as fuck sister, right before I killed her like the mangy mutt that she was. So, tell me something new, you ugly bitch." Pluto's smile was so big at this point that I could see every single one of her nasty yellow teeth.

"Well, motherfucker, you want something new? I got something to-"

A commotion near the barn distracted Pluto. We both looked over to see that Nevin had somehow broken free of his ropes. He stood behind one of the women in the circle, his hands wrapped tightly around her neck.

"Fucking try something, and I'll snap her fucking head off her body, understand?" Nevin winked at me like some whore at a church picnic. "You!" he pointed towards an irate Pluto. "Unlock Paul's cuffs, now!"

Pluto turned to me, her fist's clenched, her eyes nearing rolling back into her head.

"Come unlock these cuffs, Cunt, before your sister ends up like that *bastard* of a kid you had." I said with a grin, mocking her.

Pluto walked slowly back towards me after Nevin used his nails to dig into her captive sister's cheek. I didn't allow Pluto to use her key on the cuffs, I grabbed her by the hair with my free hand, slamming her face into the pipe. Her four other sisters gasped loudly, taking steps towards me, ready to pounce.

"Don't fucking move another inch!" Nevin demanded, punching the woman he had hostage in the lower back. The women backed off after hearing her cries. I used my free hand to pick up the razor blade covered baseball bat, using it like a cheese crater on Pluto's ugly fucking face.

"Maybe this will help." I whispered as I continued running the bat across her cheeks, nose, and gaping mouth hole. Huge chunks of flesh stared falling into my lap, most of it being her nose and lips. The fucking bitch screamed like was giving birth while her sisters looked on, helplessly.

I took the thick end of the bat and rammed it into Pluto's mouth, then began twisting it around and around. Her screams were muffled by her tongue being shredded, and the girth of the bat being forced down her throat. By the time Pluto's eyes went white, the bat had been inserted a good eight or nine inches. It was interesting to see the razor blades sticking out of her neck in random spots. I pushed her body off my lap, then grabbed the key to the cuffs.

"Thanks, that was fun." I spit on her corpse as I pulled myself up using the pipe. A loud crunching sound meant that Nevin had just snapped the neck of his hostage. The remaining girls turned to him as their sister landed face first in the mud.

"Hey, ladies, he's all yours."

Nevin's eyes grew large, realizing quickly just how fucked he was about to be. I walked back up the porch and into the living room, finding the Beretta with the two extra clips and the hunting knife. The sounds of Nevin screaming from outside were like hearing the sound of a running stream on a cool spring morning. I used my pointer fingers as if I were a conductor at a fancy, New York orchestra, I even hummed along. I went upstairs to finish off the children, hoping Nevin lived long enough to keep the remaining girls distracted until I could deal with them myself. I opened the bedroom door, expecting to hear the headache inducing screams, but there was only silence.

Once the light from the hall entered the room, I could see the large rats nibbling away, their greedy little mouths full of flesh. "Well, fuck, what irresponsible mothers." I shrugged, about to close the door behind me, when I heard a whimper behind the bedroom door. I looked around the door to see the baby with the coal black hair, the same as mine when I was her age. I kneeled down, scooping up the uneaten baby in my arms. I thought about tossing her down the stairs, wondering how many steps she would have to hit before her head popped off. The baby girl cooed loudly, smiling at me as she reached for my face.

"You smell like ass. Maybe I should drown you in a pond. It may be doing you a favor." The baby girl continued reaching up towards my face, her eyes darker than the most untenanted abyss.

"Mary-Ann." I whispered with a smile.

I walked back down the steps, wrapping Mary-Ann in an old army jacket. I pulled the pistol from my waistline before walking back out the front door. The women had finished off Nevin in a particularly brutal fashion. They eviscerated him, his large and small intestines had been stretched across the pig pen like some kind of fucked up Christmas decoration. As I walked closer, I noticed his head was missing from his nude body, along with his cock and balls. The four remaining women stood amongst the macabre and gruesome scene, almost in some sort of fucking trance. I picked out the prettiest of the four, shooting the other three in the back of their heads. The last remaining was a petite woman with greasy brown hair, and a *mildly* pretty face. She stared up at me, waiting for me to end her fucking life, but I didn't.

"Take the baby and find the keys to that car." I nodded at an ugly red car parked next to the barn with a tarp thrown lazily over top of it. I expected resistance, but the girl nodded, taking Mary-Ann in her arms. "Not that it matters, but what is your fucking name?"

The woman turned away sheepishly. "It's Mimas, that's my name."

I cringed slightly, causing her to blush from embarrassment. "That's a fucking awful name, just so you're aware. How old are you, Mimas?" I didn't necessarily want to play twenty questions with the whore, but I needed to know who it was that would be by my side until they were more useful lying face first in the nearest ditch.

"I'm sixteen, sir."

I looked around at the fucking disembowelment that Mimas had been apart of just a few minutes prior to our conversation. This girl was tiny, and she was young, but it didn't stop her from ripping off a man's cock and balls before shoving them up his ass.

"Go and get the keys to that car, we need to get on the road after I torch this fucking place."

Mimas looked up at the house, then back at me.

"Now!" I commanded loud enough that Mary-Ann's eyes shot open from the nap she was taking. Mimas nodded as she did what she was told. I found an old gas can next to the generator beside the house, it was full enough to get the job done. Mimas held on to Mary-Ann as we drove down the overgrown gravel driveway, the farmhouse burning behind us.

CHAPTER TEN

THE WOMAN WITH THE SCARS

"WHAT'S THE COUNT?" DEPUTY Logan asked, pulling out his pocket notebook.

Deputy Mills turned to him, the smoke from the extinguished fire causing his eyes to dry out.

"It's too early to talk about the inside of the house, but around seven found so far around the outside. It's mostly female remains. Two males were found, one was torn up pretty bad. I have to say, this shit is next level fucked up. I mean, what in the hell happened here?" Deputy Mills had never seen anything like this, nor had any of the other officers on scene.

"Let's keep it professional, Mills. You don't want Sheriff Rhea showing up and hearing you talk like that, do you?" Mills shook his head, standing up a bit straighter.

"Go check with the fire chief and see if they've determined how that fire got started, and if they've found anything else amongst the rubble." Mills nodded at Logan, tipping his hat as he turned to go and find the fire chief.

"What a fucking nightmare." Logan muttered to himself, hearing another car door close from behind him. He turned to see Sheriff Rhea walking towards him, her dark aviator sunglasses pushed up on her nose, her hat tilted down low on her head, and the limp she's had since the day Logan joined the department.

"What do you know so far?" Sheriff Rhea asked, only staring at the smoldering pile of ash and remaining foundation of the old farmhouse.

Logan cleared his throat, hoping like hell to not say the wrong thing in front of the Sheriff. "We're still determining the cause of the fire, but there were multiple casualties on site, including two young men with out of state ID's." Logan wondered if the Sheriff would remove her glasses to reveal her ghostly white, left eye.

Sheriff Rhea stood with her hands on her hips, turning her head slowly to the left, then to the right. "You're familiar with the young ladies that lived out here, aren't you, Sheriff?" Logan asked, regrettably.

Rhea stood in silence for a few more moments before pulling off her sunglasses. Logan had known the Sheriff going on four years, give or take a couple of months. He had grown pretty accustomed to the Sheriff's strict, hard-nosed manner, and no-nonsense ways. He, of course, had no choice otherwise. But those scars, those deep, horrendous looking scars on the left side of her head and face. He always felt a sense of unease when he looked at them for more than a few seconds.

He'd heard a rumor a couple years back that the Sheriff was covered from head to toe in deep, nasty scars that looked like animals had chewed on her. But he pushed all that shit into the back of his gray-matter and focused on the task at hand.

"I came to see these girls from time to time, helped them get on. They lived out here by themselves, naked amongst the horrors that surrounded them. These girls survived the best way they knew how, fighting against those who saw fit to do them harm." Sheriff Rhea cleared her throat, pushing her sunglasses back up her nose. "I want the entire area blocked off, from here, to that old cabin in the clearing. You got that?" Sheriff Rhea turned, limping slowly towards the group of coroners in white hazmat suits, picking up scattered body parts near the front of the house.

"The two males that were found, let me see them."

One of the coroners pointed to a pair of stretchers near a black van, two body bags resting atop of them. Sheriff Rhea limped as quickly as she could over to the bags, unzipping the first to see a young man's severed head, resting on his bloody chest. "Lord, have mercy on us all." Sheriff Rhea whispered, zipping up the first bag. She felt her heart racing as she opened the second bag.

"It's not him." Rhea took a deep breath as relief set over her. *He must still be in the cellar. He fucking has to be down there still. There would be no reason for them to let him go. They were always so careful, so smart about him. That's why they had the dart gun, that's why I had them take precautions. They believed they were worshiping the god of pain; they were happy doing the weird shit that they did as I turned a blind eye. This was all for me, they just didn't know that. They were innocent. So, what if it was my idea to keep him down there, where else was I supposed to have him locked up for the rest of his life? It couldn't have been prison, that would have been too fucking easy for him. He deserved to stay locked away in the dark until the day he fucking died! But what if he's alive down there? What if the fire never reached the cellar? They would dig through all this shit and find him; they wouldn't know who he was, and they would just let him out. I can't let them-*

"Sheriff Rhea? Ma'am? Are you alright? I've been calling out to you for over a minute."

Rhea looked up, Deputy Logan and Mills were standing directly in front of her. Had she said anything out loud? Did they hear anything?

"I was just thinking, how about you two go off and do the same." Sheriff Rhea huffed loudly, limping back towards the old farmhouse.

"Well, Sheriff, we wanted to let you know that the city inspector stopped by with the blueprint of the farmhouse. From what I'm seeing, there is a cellar below the basement. From what the inspector was telling me, it was used as a meat locker over a hundred years ago. The only reason I'm bringing it up is because there could be people trapped down there."

Sheriff Rhea stopped in her tracks, then turned a finger on Deputy Logan. "No one touches anything without my say so, understand?"

Logan and Mills shot a quick glance to one another before nodding their heads in agreement.

"Anything else you want us to do, Sheriff?" Mills asked, clearing his throat. Sheriff

Rhea opened the door to her police cruiser, turning one last time to her deputies. "Yeah, find out the make and model of the car that those two outsiders showed up in. Once you find out, call *me* immediately, understood?"

Mills and Logan nodded once more.

Sheriff Rhea put the cruiser in drive, spinning rocks as she shot down the old driveway. "How could I have been so stupid? I should have found out about the car those boys were driving the second I found out that they were dead! Stupid fucking girls must have gotten sloppy and brought those outsiders in. Where they going to use them the same way they were using Paul? They didn't clear that shit with me, they didn't say a fucking word about it."

She didn't know if she had been rambling on to herself, or if it was a voice in her head. She pulled a small bottle of pills from the center console, popping the lid off and throwing back more than the recommended dose.

***

"What's your name?" The sight of Luna looking down on her was all she could remember. "Pluto, go get anything we can use from inside the house."

Pluto Stopped, gulping loudly. "The daddies are dead, you know that! Now hurry up and go get whatever you can find!"

Pluto ran from the barn for the first time in her short life. "My sister is going to find some supplies to help you. Our daddies took care of those pigs, had to stitch them up after they would get snagged on the barbed wire fence. Those stupid hogs didn't mean anything when they attacked you. They're just a little territorial, that's all." Luna stroked her matted hair like she was a doll.

"My neck, I think it might be broken, please, please help me."

Luna didn't stop smiling, she just continued running her fingers through her hair.

"The vet is stopping by tomorrow afternoon to drop off some more supplies for the daddies. We'll get him to come fix up what we can't fix today. Sad part is, we may have to keep him here with us until you're better. I don't mean to frighten you, but you have a lot more than a silly old broken neck."

The girl lying on the barn floor began to cry.

"It's alright. Don't cry, we'll take care of you. Now, what's your name?" The girl on the ground whispered something as she started to lose consciousness.

"Mary-Ann."

Luna smiled. "I like that name, it's really pretty. But my sisters and I have special names that our daddies gave us, would you like me to give *you* a special name?" Luna thought for a moment, still running her dirty fingers through Mary-Ann's hair. "I got it, how about, Rhea? Do you like that name?"

Mary-Ann forced a smile, before slipping into darkness.

***

"Sheriff Rhea, come in, Sheriff Rhea!" The sound of the police radio on the dash of the cruiser was enough to snap Rhea from her daydream.

"This is Sheriff Rhea, go ahead." The voice on the other end was Deputy Logan, a man that Rhea had grown annoyed with quite easily. Logan was a do-gooder, always questioning Rhea's decisions.

"Sheriff, we got back the make and model of the car those boys were driving." After writing down the license plate number and the make and model of the car, Rhea pushed harder on the gas pedal.

"I'm coming for you, Paul. And when I find you, you're going to wish you had died in that fucking house."

EPILOGUE

I TURNED ON THE car radio after tossing out all the bullshit from the backseat. "Is this music nowadays?" I asked the babysitter I had taken from the pig farm.

Mimas shrugged her shoulders, looking out the window at the passing trees. "I've never been in a moving car before, it's kind of fun." she smiled, turning in her head to look in the backseat at Mary-Ann. I took one hand off the wheel and used it to punch Mimas in the side of the fucking head.

"You're not here for '*fun*', you dumb bitch."

Mimas held her head with both hands, crying into her lap. "You are here to keep that baby quiet, and happy, understand? You're not here to fucking enjoy yourself! If I get even the slightest fucking feeling that you're even the least bit chipper, I'll bash your fucking skull in, got it?"

She cried louder as I grabbed the back of her neck, bashing her face into the dashboard.

"Wake the fucking baby up and I'll toss you the fuck out!"

She took a few deep breaths, wiping the blood from her nose and forehead. "I'm sorry." she whispered, looking over at me with big, puppy dog eyes. I almost felt like telling her how much I fucking hated dogs.

"It's fine, you're still learning how to be a good little bitch, and I understand that. Now look, I'm only going to tell you this once, understand? If at any time during our little adventure that you decide to get brave and come at me, I'll kill that baby right in front of you before I cut your fucking tits off, understood?"

Mimas nodded, turning again to check on Mary-Ann, who was still wrapped comfortably in the old army jacket.

"This is typically the part where I tell you that we need to lay low until I can figure out what in the fuck to do next. But I'll tell you what, bitch, I'm tired as fuck of lying low. It's about time I get back out there, it's about goddamn time that the world remembers just who in the fuck I am."

I tilted the rearview mirror to get a good look at Mary-Ann, wondering just how useful she would be to me later in life. Suddenly, I began thinking about the *real* Mary-Ann, and the awful fucking death that *she* brought upon herself. I'd give anything to see that bitch just one more time.

"You know something, cunt? I haven't had my dick in something as ugly as you since that time one of your bitch sisters tossed me a dead cat. I wasn't sure if they expected me to eat it, or fuck it, so I did both."

Mimas tensed up at the feeling of my hand on her leg.

"Are you scared? That would be strange if you were. I mean, you lived in a commune of nasty fucking whores your entire life." I started feeling angry but decided that my energy was best placed somewhere else. "Put your mouth on cock, I'll teach you how to suck it." I laughed as we drove happily into the sunset.

TO BE CONTIUNED...

Acknowledgements

I'd like to thank my writing troupe (even thought they have no idea that they even are one) That would be Chuck Nasty, Daisy Rae, Asher Dark, Nick Scarbrough, and S.S Hughes.

Also, Thank you, Jason Nickey, you're a great writing partner, and an even better friend.

Thank you, Chrissy and Scott Cecil, of Hat Girl. LLC for all the killer merch.

And thank you to all the Violence on the Meek fans out there, I wouldn't be doing this if not for you.

ABOUT THE AUTHOR

Stuart bray was born on September 11th, 1991, in Louisville, Kentucky he grew up with the love and fascination I'm 4 movies and storytelling Stuart wrote his first scary story at the age of seven, titled "Two kids and an alien" he still resides in rural Kentucky with his wife and two children. Stuart is also the host of the murder shed podcast available on all podcast streaming platforms. He is a huge hockey fan and cheers for the Toronto Maple Leafs. You can follow him on Twitter and Instagram @stuartbray91 every little flaw is the second book written by the author, his first book "The Heretic" is available on Amazon.com

ALSO BY

Novellas:

The Heretic

Every Little Flaw

Cotton Candy

His Name's Vicious

Violence On The Meek

Violence On The Meek 2: Anointing Of The Sick

Violence On The Meek 3: Hybristophilia

Broken Pieces Of June

White Trash: Broken Pieces Of June 2

June: Broken Pieces Of June 3

Broken: The June Trilogy (Featuring the short story 'The Freak)

The Ballad Of Harley Heck

Sour Under The Flesh

Obscurus, 1939 (As Stuart Drake)

The Boys Of Barren County

Collections:

I'll Bury You Tomorrow

Collaborations:

Hillbillies And Homicidal Maniacs (With Jason Nickey)

Hillbillies And Homicidal Maniacs Vol 2: Horror In The Holler (With Jason Nickey)

When The Mockingbird Sings (With Jason Nickey)

Sludge (With Jason Nickey and Chuck Nasty)

Ensuring Your Place In Hell (With Stephen Cooper and Otis Bateman)

Made in the USA
Middletown, DE
01 June 2024